Victor Pelevin

Born 1962 in Moscow, Victor Pelevin has established a
reputation as one of the most brilliant of the younger
generation of Russian writers. His work has already appeared
in the most prestigious magazines of Russian literature, with
Omon Ra published in *Znamye* and *The Yellow Arrow* in
Novy Mir, as well as being translated, to date, into French,
German and Japanese.

Pelevin is one of the few writers in Russia who is writing
seriously about what is happening in the country today, albeit
with a style of ironic detachment which has become a
characteristic mark of his generation – one born too late
to be confronted by the choice of whether to accept,
or reject, the orthodoxies of the official system. Drawing on
strands as various as science fiction and oriental religion,
Pelevin's work is both critically acclaimed in Russia as well
as being popular with readers.

Omon Ra was among the novels nominated for the 1993
Russian Booker Prize. In fact, Victor Pelevin was awarded the
supporting prize of that year's competition, the so-called
"Little Booker", for the best volume of short stories published
in Russian between 1991 and 1993, for his collection *The Blue
Lantern*.

Andrew Bromfield

Andrew Bromfield was born in Hull, and graduated in Russian
Studies from the University of Sussex. His varied career has
included lecturing in Russian for 12 years and teaching English
in Yerevan, Soviet Armenia. From 1988 to 1993 he lived and
worked in Moscow, where he was involved in setting up *Glas*,
an English-language journal of contemporary Russian writing,
of which he was co-editor. He has translated widely from
Russian, in both poetry and prose.

Omon Ra

with the novella *The Yellow Arrow*

By Victor Pelevin

Translated from the Russian by Andrew Bromfield

Harbord Publishing

Published by Harbord Publishing Limited
58 Harbord Street, London SW6 6PL.

Omon Ra and *The Yellow Arrow* © Victor Pelevin, 1992.
Translation © Andrew Bromfield, 1994.
All rights reserved. The moral rights of the author and
translator have been asserted.

British Library Cataloguing in Publication data.
A CIP record for this book is available from the British Library.

Omon Ra was originally published in Russian by Text Publishers,
Moscow, 1992.

Printed in England by Hartnolls Limited, Bodmin, Cornwall.

The publishers express their gratitude to Natalya Perova in Moscow
and Celia Duncan in London for help in preparation of this book.

The translator expresses his special thanks to
Elena Sergeievna Gordon for her invaluable contribution
to his understanding of Russian language, literature and art,
including the present texts.

ISBN 1 899414 00 2

Omon Ra

For the Heroes of the Soviet Cosmos

1

Omon is not a particularly common name, and perhaps not the best there is. It was my father's idea. He worked in the police all his life and wanted me to be a policeman too.

"Listen to me, Ommy," he used to say to me when he'd been drinking, "if you join the police, with a name like that... then if you join the Party..."

Although my father had occasionally shot at people, he wasn't really vicious by nature, in his heart he was a cheerful and sympathetic man. He loved me a lot, and hoped that life would at least grant me the achievements it had denied him. What he really wanted was to get hold of a plot of land somewhere near Moscow and start growing beetroot and cucumbers on it – not so that he could sell them at the market or eat them (though that too), but so that he could strip to the waist, slice into the earth with his spade and watch the red worms and the other underground life wriggling about, so that he could cart barrowloads of dung from one end of the holiday village to the other, stopping at other people's gates to swap a few jokes. When he realised he would never get any of this, he began to hope that at least one of the Krivomazov brothers would lead a long and happy life (my elder brother, Ovir, whom my father had wanted to make into a diplomat, died of meningitis at the age of eleven, and all I remember about him is that he had a long oblong birthmark on his forehead).

My father's plans on my behalf failed to inspire me with any real confidence – after all, he himself was a Party man, and he had a perfectly good Russian name, Matvei, but all he had earned for his efforts was a miserly pension and a lonely, drunken old age.

I don't remember my mother too well. The only memory I have is of my drunken father in his uniform trying to pull his pistol out of its holster while she clutched at his arms, her hair all messed up, and shouted: "Matvei, come to your senses!"

She died when I was still very young, and I was raised by an aunt, and went to see my father at weekends. He usually had a red and puffy look, and the medal he was so proud of hung crooked on his soiled pyjama jacket. There was a bad smell in his room, and hanging on the wall was a reproduction of Michelangelo's fresco, 'The Creation', with Adam lying on his back and a bearded God floating above him stretching out his mighty hand to touch the frail human one. This picture had a strangely profound effect on my father, it clearly reminded him of something from the past. I usually sat on the floor of his room and played with a toy train set, while he snored on the fold-down divan. Sometimes he would wake up and peer at me for a while through screwed-up eyes, then he would hang over the edge of the divan, propping himself against the floor, and stretch out a large veinous hand that I was supposed to shake.

"So what's your surname?"

"Krivomazov," I would reply, faking a shy smile, and he would pat me on the head and feed me sweets; he ran through the whole routine so mechanically that it didn't even disgust me.

There's almost nothing I can say about my aunt – she was quite indifferent to me and made sure that I spent most of my free time in various summer camps for young pioneers, and extended day school groups.

Everything I remember from my childhood is linked in one way or another with a dream of the sky. Of course, all this wasn't the very beginning of my life, before this there was a long bright room full of other children and large plastic cubes scattered haphazardly about the floor; there were the ice-bound steps of the wooden slide that I plodded up with eager haste; there were the frost-cracked models of young mountaineers made of painted plaster in the yard, and lots more besides. But I can't really say that it was me who saw all this; in early child-hood (as, perhaps, after death), a person extends in all direct-ions at the same time, so we can say he still doesn't exist yet – the personality comes into being later, when an attachment to some particular direction appears.

I lived not far from the 'Cosmos' cinema. Our district was dominated by a metal rocket standing on a tapering column of solid titanium smoke, like some huge scimitar thrust into the ground. But funnily enough, it wasn't this rocket that marked the beginning of my personality, it was the wooden aeroplane in the small children's playground beside my block. It wasn't exactly an aeroplane, more a toy house with two windows, and during some repair work someone had nailed on a pair of wings and a tail made from the boards of a fence that had been pulled down, then covered the whole thing with green paint and decorated it with a few large reddish stars. There was room inside for two or three people, and there was a small attic with a little triangular window that looked out on to the wall of the military enlistment office – by unwritten agreement of the entire yard, this attic was regarded as the pilot's cabin, and when the plane was shot down, those who were sitting in the body of the fuselage jumped first, and only afterwards, when the earth was already roaring up towards the windows, could the pilot follow them – if, of course, he had time. I always tried to be the pilot, and I could actually see the sky and the clouds and the Earth floating by below, where the brick wall of the military enlistment office should have been, with the whiskery violets and dusty cacti peering forlornly out of its windows.

I really loved films about airmen, and one of these films provided the most powerful experience of my childhood. On a cosmically dark December evening, I switched on my aunt's television and there on the screen was an aeroplane swaying its wings, with an ace of spades on its side and a cross on its fuselage. I leant down towards the screen, and immediately it was filled with a close-up of the cabin section. Behind the thick panes of glass a subhuman face smiled in goggles like a mountain skier's and a helmet with gleaming ebonite ear-pieces. The pilot raised an open hand clad in a glove with a long black sleeve and waved to me. Then the screen was filled with an inside view of another plane: two fliers in fur-lined jackets were sitting at identical control columns and peering through the metal-framed plexiglass, following the convolutions of the enemy fighter flying close beside them.

"M-109," said one flier to the other, "they'll bring us down." The other, with a handsome emaciated face, nodded.

"I don't hold it against you," he said, clearly continuing an interrupted conversation. "But just remember: this thing between you and Varya had better be for life... To the grave!"

At that point I stopped taking in the action on the screen. I was struck by the sudden thought, or not even a thought, merely its faintly registered shadow – as though the actual thought had floated past close to my head, only catching it with its edge – that if I'd just been able to glance at the screen and see the world from the cabin where the two fliers in fur-lined jackets were sitting, then there was nothing to prevent me from getting into this or any other cabin without the help of the television, because flight is no more than a set of sensations, the most important of which I'd already learned to fake, sitting in the attic of the winged hut with the red stars, staring at the enlistment office wall that was where the sky should be, and making quiet droning noises with my mouth.

This vague realisation struck me so hard that I watched the rest of the film without paying proper attention, only getting involved in the television reality when the screen was filled with smoke trails or a row of enemy planes standing on the ground hurtling up towards me. "That means," I thought, "I can look out from inside myself like looking out of a plane, it doesn't really matter at all where you look out from, what matters is what you see..." From that time on, as I wandered along some winter-time street, I often imagined that I was flying in a plane over snow-covered fields; as I turned a corner, I inclined my head, and the world obediently tilted right or left.

All the same, the person that I could with real certainty call myself only took shape later, and gradually. I think the first glimpse of my true personality was the moment when I realised I could aspire beyond the thin blue film of the sky into the black abyss of space. It happened the same winter, one evening when I was strolling around the Exhibition of Economic Achievements in another corner of Moscow. I was walking along a dark and empty snow-covered alley: suddenly on my left I heard this droning, like a huge telephone ringing. I turned – and saw him.

Sitting there in empty space, leaning back as though in an armchair, he was slowly drifting forwards, and the tubes behind him were straightening out at the same slow pace. The glass of his helmet was black, and the only bright spot on it was a triangular highlight, but I knew he could see me. He could have been dead for centuries. His arms were stretched out confidently towards the stars, and his legs were so obviously not in need of any support, that I realised once and for ever that only weightlessness could give man genuine freedom – which, incidentally, is why all my life I've only been bored by all those Western radio voices and those books by various Solzhenitsyns. In my heart, of course, I loathed a state whose silent menace obliged every group of people who came together, even if only for a few seconds, to imitate zealously the vilest and bawdiest individual among them; but since I realised that peace and freedom were unattainable on earth, my spirit aspired aloft, and everything that my chosen path required ceased to conflict with my conscience, because my conscience was calling me out into space, and was not much interested in what was happening on earth.

What I saw in front of me was simply a spotlit mosaic on the wall of an exhibition pavilion, a picture of a cosmonaut in open space, but it told me more in an instant than the dozens of books I'd read before that day. I stood there looking at it, until suddenly I felt someone looking at me.

Glancing round, I saw behind my back a rather strange-looking boy of my own age – he was wearing a leather helmet with gleaming ebonite ear-phones, and there were plastic swimming goggles dangling round his neck. He was a little taller than me and probably a few months older. As he entered the area illuminated by the spotlight, he raised an open hand in a black glove, stretched his lips into a cold smile, and for an instant there stood before me the flyer from the cabin of that fighter-plane marked with the ace of spades.

He was called Mitiok. It turned out that we lived close to one another, although we went to different schools. Mitiok had his doubts about many things, but he knew one thing for certain. He knew that first he would become a pilot, and then he would fly to the Moon.

2

There's obviously some strange correspondence between the general outline of a life and that stream of petty events in which a person is constantly involved and regards as insignificant. I can now see quite clearly that the course of my own life was already set, determined before I had even begun to think seriously about the way I wanted it to turn out: I was even given a glimpse of it in simplified form. Perhaps it was an echo of the future. Or perhaps those things which we take for echoes of the future are actually its seeds, falling into the soil of life at the very moment which in distant retrospect comes to seem like an echo out of the future.

To be brief, the summer after seventh grade was hot and dusty. All I remember of the first half of it are long bicycle rides on one of the highways outside Moscow. I attached a special rattle to the rear of my bike, a 'Sport' semi-racer; it consisted of a piece of thick paper folded over several times and fastened to the frame with a clothes-peg – as I rode along, the paper struck against the spokes and made a quick, quiet whirring noise, like the sound of an aero-engine. Time and again as I hurtled down a tarmac incline, I became a fighter-plane closing in on its target, and by no means always a Soviet one. But I wasn't to blame for that, it was just that at the beginning of summer I'd heard someone sing a stupid song which included the words: "Swift as a bullet my Phantom roars into the clear blue sky." I must confess that for all the song's stupidity, which I realised perfectly well, I was moved to the depths of my soul. What other words can I remember? "I see a smoke trail in the sky... My Texas home is far away..." And there was a father, and a mother, and someone called Mary, a very real person, because she was actually named in the song.

I was back in Moscow for the middle of July, and then Mitiok's parents got us places in the 'Rocket' camp. It was a typical summer camp for children in the South, maybe even a little better than most. I really only remember the first few days we spent there – but that was when everything that became so important later happened. In the train Mitiok and I ran through the carriages, throwing all the bottles we could find down the toilets – they fell on the railway tracks rushing by beyond the tiny hatch and burst soundlessly; the stupid song that was stuck in my head gave this simple game the flavour of the struggle for the liberation of Vietnam. The next day the entire contingent for the camp, who had all travelled in the same train, was unloaded at a wet railroad station in a provincial town to be counted and loaded into trucks. We drove for a long time along a road which looped between mountains, then on our right the sea appeared and little houses of various colours came drifting towards us. We piled out on to an asphalted parade-square and were led up steps flanked by cypress trees to a low glass-walled building on the top of the hill. This was the dining-hall, where a cold lunch was waiting for us, although it was already supper-time – we had arrived several hours later than expected. The food was pretty bad – thin soup with macaroni stars, tough chicken with rice, and tasteless stewed fruit.

Hanging down from the ceiling of the dining-hall on threads covered with tacky-looking kitchen glue were cardboard models of spaceships. I stared at one of them in admiration – the anonymous artist had gone to a great deal of effort and covered it all over with the letters "USSR". The setting sun looking in on it through the window suddenly seemed to me like the headlight of a train in the metro as it emerges from the darkness of the tunnel. Somehow I felt sad.

But Mitiok was in a happy mood and felt like talking:

"In the twenties they had one kind of spaceship," he said, jerking his fork up into the air, "in the thirties they were different, in the fifties they were different again, and so on..."

"What kind of spaceships were there in the twenties?" I asked listlessly.

Mitiok thought for a moment.

"Alexei Tolstoy had these huge metal eggs powered by explosions at miniscule time intervals," he said. "That was the basic principle, but there could be lots of variations."

"But they never really flew," I said.

"Neither do these," he answered, pointing to the model we were discussing as it swayed gently in the draught.

I finally got his point, although couldn't really have put it into words. The only space in which the starships of the communist future had flown (incidentally, when I first came across the word "starship" in the science fantasy books I used to like so much, I thought it came from the red stars on the sides of Soviet space craft) was the Soviet psyche, just as the dining-hall we were sitting in was the cosmic space in which the ships launched by the previous camp contingent would go on ploughing their furrows through time up there above the dining tables, even when the creators of the cardboard fleet were long gone. This thought filtered through the peculiar indescribable ennui I always suffered after the boiled fruit at the camp, and then I suddenly had a strange idea.

"I used to like making plastic aeroplane models," I said, "from the kits. Especially military planes."

"So did I," said Mitiok, "but that was a long time ago."

"I liked the East German kits. But there were no pilots in ours. They looked stupid, because the cockpits were always empty."

"That's right," said Mitiok. "What made you think of that?"

"I was just thinking," I said, pointing my fork at the starship hanging just in front of our table, "whether there's anyone inside there or not?"

"I don't know," said Mitiok. "It's an interesting question, alright."

The camp was set on the gentle slope of a hill, and its lower section formed a kind of park. Mitiok had disappeared, and I went off that way on my own: in a few minutes I was in a long, deserted avenue of cypress trees, where it was already half dark.

Wire netting stretched alongside the asphalt footpath, and on the netting there hung large sheets of plywood with hand-drawn posters on them. On the first there was a young pioneer with a simple Russian face, staring ahead of him as he pressed a brass bugle with a small flag to his thigh. On the second the same pioneer had a drum hanging on a strap and was holding the drumsticks. He was there again on the third panel, gazing into the distance in the same way from under a hand raised in salute. The next sheet of plywood was about twice as wide as the rest and very tall – probably about three metres. It was in two colours: on the right, the side from which I was slowly approaching, it was red, and further away from me it was white, and these two colours were separated by the ragged edge of a wave invading the white surface and leaving a red trail in its wake. At first I couldn't understand what it was, and it was only when I came closer that I recognised the interspersed red and white blobs as the face of Lenin, with a jutting beard that looked like a battering-ram and an open mouth; Lenin had no back to his head – there was just his profile, and all of the red surface behind it was Lenin. He was like some incorporeal god rippling across the surface of the world which he had created.

I stumbled over a pot-hole in the road and shifted my gaze to the next board – it was the pioneer again, but this time wearing a space suit, with a red helmet in his hand; the helmet bore the inscription "USSR" and a pointed antenna. The next pioneer was leaning out of a rocket in flight and saluting with a hand in a heavy-duty glove. The final picture was the pioneer in a space suit, standing on the cheerful yellow surface of the Moon beside a spaceship like the cardboard rocket in the dining-hall; all that could be seen of him were his eyes, the same eyes as on the other boards, but because all the rest of his face was concealed by the helmet, they seemed filled with some inexpressible anguish.

There was the sound of swift steps behind me, and I turned round and saw Mitiok.

"There *was*," he said, as he came up to me.

"There was what?"

"Look." He held out his hand with something dark lying on the palm. I made out a little plasticine figure with its head wrapped in foil.

"There was a little cardboard chair inside, and he was sitting on it," said Mitiok.

"What, did you take the rocket in the dining-hall to pieces?" I asked him.

He nodded.

"When?"

"Just now. Ten minutes ago. The strangest thing of all is that everything in there was..." He crossed the fingers of both hands over each other to form a grid.

"In the dining-hall?"

"No, in the rocket. When they made it, they started with this little man. They made him and sat him on the chair and glued the cardboard shut all around him."

Mitiok held out a scrap of cardboard. I took it and saw painstakingly detailed drawings of instruments, handles, buttons, and even a picture on the wall.

"But the most interesting thing," Mitiok said in a thoughtful and depressed sort of voice, "is that there was no door. There was a hatch drawn on the outside, but in the same place on the inside – just some dials on the wall."

I glanced again at the scrap of cardboard and noticed a porthole through which the Earth was visible, small and blue.

"I'd like to find the man who stuck this rocket together," said Mitiok, "I'd punch his ugly face for him."

"What for?" I asked.

Mitiok didn't answer. Instead he swung back his arm in order to chuck the figure over the wire netting, but I caught his hand and asked him to give the figure to me. He didn't object, and I spent the next half hour looking for an empty cigarette pack to use as a case.

The echo of this strange discovery came back to us the next day, during the camp's quiet hour. The door opened and Mitiok's name was called; he went out into the corridor. I could hear snatches of conversation, the word "dining-hall" was repeated several times, and everything was clear. I stood up and went out into the corridor. Mitiok was there, pressed into the corner by two camp leaders – a skinny young man with a moustache and a squat ginger-haired woman.

"I was there too," I said.

The male leader looked me up and down approvingly:

"Do you want to crawl together or take turns?"

I saw he had a green bag with a gas-mask in his hand.

"How can they crawl together, Kolya, when you've only got one gas-mask?" the female leader asked timidly. "They have to take turns."

Mitiok gave me a swift glance and took a step forward.

"Put it on," said the camp leader.

Mitiok put on the gas-mask.

"Get down."

He lay on the floor.

"Move," said Kolya, clicking on his stop-watch. The floor of the corridor, which ran the full length of the building, was covered with linoleum, and when Mitiok began to crawl forward, the linoleum gave out a soft but unpleasant squeak. Of course, Mitiok took longer than the three minutes allowed by the camp leader – it wasn't even long enough for him to crawl along the corridor in one direction – but when he had come crawling back towards us, Kolya didn't force him to cover the distance again, because there were only a few minutes left to the end of quiet hour. Mitiok took off the gas-mask. His face was red and dripping with tears and sweat. Blisters had swelled up on his feet where they rubbed against the linoleum.

"Now you," said the camp-leader, handing me the wet gas-mask. "Get ready..."

There is something weird and mysterious in the way a corridor looks when you're gazing at its linoleum-spread expanses through the steamed-up lenses of a gas-mask. The floor you're lying on chills your belly and chest; you can't even see its far end, the pale ribbon of ceiling and the walls are fused together almost into a point. The gas-mask gently squeezes your face, pressing on your cheeks and forcing your lips to stretch into a kind of kiss, apparently addressed to everything around you. Before someone prods you with their foot and orders you to crawl, about twenty seconds pass: a long period of slow torment, time enough to notice all sorts of things. Take the dust – there are several transparent specks there in the crack between two sheets of linoleum; take that painted-over knot in the wood of the skirting-board; take that ant that death has transformed into two incredibly thin little petals, which has left behind it a small moist spot in the future half a metre away where the foot of a person walking down the corridor stepped just a second after the disaster.

"Go!" The command rang out above my head and I began cheerfully and earnestly crawling forward. The punishment seemed more like a joke to me, and I didn't understand why Mitiok had turned so weepy. I covered the first ten metres quick as a flash; then it got harder.

When you crawl, there's a moment at which you push off from the floor with the upper part of your foot, and the skin there is thin and delicate, and if you've nothing on your feet, you immediately get a blister from the friction. The linoleum stuck to my body, and it felt like hundreds of tiny insects were boring into my legs or like I was crawling over freshly laid asphalt. I was astonished at how slowly time was passing – at one spot on the wall there was a large watercolour of the cruiser 'Aurora' in the Black Sea, and I noticed I'd been crawl-ing past it for quite a long time, but it was still hanging there in the same place...

Then suddenly everything changed. That is, everything was just the same as before – I was crawling along the corridor in just the same way – but the pain and fatigue, passing beyond the level of endurance, seemed to switch something off inside me. Or else just the opposite – they switched something on. I noticed that all around me it was very quiet, there was only the squeaking of the linoleum under my feet, as though something was trundling along the corridor on rusty castors; outside the windows, way below me, the sea was murmuring, and somewhere even further away, maybe beyond the sea, a loud-speaker was singing with children's voices.

"*Beautiful yonder, do not hurt me so,*
Do not be cruel..."

Life was a tender green miracle; the sky was clear and still, the sun was shining – and in the very centre of this world stood the two-storey dormitory building, and inside it was the long corridor, along which I was crawling in a gas-mask. It was all so natural, and at the same time so painful and absurd, that I began to cry inside my rubber snout, feeling glad that my real face was hidden from the camp leaders, and especially from the chinks round the doors, through which dozens of eyes were gazing at my glory and my shame.

After a few more metres my tears dried up and I joined in the song, very quietly, maybe without actually making any sound at all:

"*From the pure source into the beautiful yonder,*
Into the beautiful yonder I chart my path."

The bright brassy note of a trumpet drifted over the camp –

that was réveille. I stopped and opened my eyes. There were three metres left to the end of the corridor. On the dark grey wall in front of me hung a shelf, with a yellow globe of the Moon standing on it; through the steamy glass smeared with tears it appeared blurred and indistinct, as though it wasn't standing on a shelf, but hanging in a grey void.

3

The first time in my life I drank wine was during the winter when I was fourteen. It was in a garage that Mitiok took me to – his brother, a pensive long-haired type who had tricked his way out of army service, worked there as a watchman. The garage was on a large fenced-off lot stacked with concrete slabs, and Mitiok and I spent quite a long time clambering over them, sometimes ending up in astonishing places entirely screened off from the rest of reality which were like the compartments of a long-abandoned spaceship of which only the carcass was left, strangely resembling a heap of concrete slabs. What's more, the street lamps beyond the crooked wooden fence burned with a mysterious and unearthly light, and a few small stars hung in the pure empty sky – in short, if not for the empty bottles of cheap booze and the frozen streams of urine, we would have been surrounded by cosmic space.

Mitiok suggested going in to warm ourselves up, and we set off towards the ribbed aluminium hemisphere of the garage, which also had something cosmic about it. Inside it was dark: we could make out the dim forms of cars that smelt of petrol. In the corner was a planking hut with a glazed window, built up against the wall: there was a light on inside it. Mitiok and I squeezed our way inside, sat down on a narrow, uncomfortable bench and silently drank our fill of tea from a battered tin saucepan. Mitiok's brother was smoking long hand-rolled cigarettes with cardboard roaches, and looking through an old issue of *Young Technology* magazine, and he didn't acknowledge our presence at all. Mitiok pulled a bottle out from under the bench, smacked it down on to the cement floor and asked:

"Want some?"

I nodded, although I felt uneasy about it. Mitiok filled the glass I'd just been drinking tea from right up to the brim with a dark-red liquid and held it out to me. As though I was trying to get the hang of some new procedure, I grasped the glass, raised it to my mouth and drank, amazed at how little effort was required to do something for the first time. While Mitiok and his brother finished off the rest, I paid close attention to my own sensations, but there was nothing happening to me. I picked up the magazine that had been put down, opened it at random and was faced with a double spread of drawings of flying machines whose names you were supposed to guess. I liked one better than the others – it was an American aeroplane with wings that could function as a rotor during take-off – and there was a small rocket with a cabin for the pilot, but I didn't get a proper look at that, because without saying a word or even raising his eyes, Mitiok's brother grabbed the magazine out of my hands. In order not to show I was offended, I moved over and sat at the table, on which a glass jar with a water-heating element protruding from it stood among shrivelling pieces of cheap salami.

I suddenly felt disgusted to think that I was sitting in this lousy little closet that smelt like a garbage-tip, disgusted by the fact that I'd just drunk cheap port from a dirty glass, that the entire immense country in which I lived was made up of lots and lots of these lousy little closets where there was a smell of garbage and people had just been drinking cheap port, and most important of all – it was painful to think that these very same stinking little closets were the settings for those multi-coloured arrays of lights that made me catch my breath in the evenings when I happened to look out of some window set high above the twilight capital. And it all seemed particularly painful in comparison with the beautiful American flying machine in the magazine.

I lowered my eyes to the newspaper which was spread over the table – it was a mass of grease spots, holes burned by cigarette butts and ring-marks left by glasses and saucers. The headlines were strangely frightening, with an inhuman cheerfulness and power: it was a long time since anyone had stood in their way, but still they went on beating at the empty air, and if you were drunk (and I noticed that I already was, but I didn't attach any importance to it), you could easily happen just to be in the wrong place and get your loitering soul crushed under some 'Major Objective of the Current Plan' or some 'Greeting from the Cotton Harvesters'. The room around me was suddenly totally strange; Mitiok was watching me carefully. He caught my eye, winked, and with a tongue that moved thickly, he asked:

"What about it, we gonna fly to the Moon?"

I nodded, and my eyes came to rest on a small column titled 'News from Orbit!' The bottom of the text had been torn off, and all that was left of the column were the words "Twenty-eight days..." in bold type. But this was still enough – I understood immediately and closed my eyes: yes, it was true, perhaps the burrows in which our lives were spent really were dark and dirty, and perhaps we ourselves were well suited to these burrows, but in the blue sky above our heads, up among the thinly scattered stars there were special, artificial points of gleaming light, creeping unhurriedly through the constellations, points created here in the land of Soviets, among the vomit, empty bottles and stench of tobacco smoke, points built here out of steel, semiconductors and electricity, and now flying through space. And every one of us, even the blue-faced alcoholic we had passed on the way here, huddling like a toad in a snowdrift, even Mitiok's brother, and of course Mitiok and myself – we all had our own little embassy up there in the cold pure blueness.

I ran outside and stood there for ages, swallowing my tears as I stared up at the bluish-yellow, improbably-near orb of the Moon in the transparent winter sky.

4

I don't remember the exact moment when I decided to enroll in military college, probably because this decision had ripened in my soul, and in Mitiok's, long before we graduated from high school. For a little while we faced the problem of choice – there were a lot of flying schools around the country – but we made our minds up very quickly once we saw a coloured double-page insert in the magazine *Soviet Aviation*, all about life in the Lunar Village at the Maresiev Red Banner Flying School in Zaraisk. We immediately felt as though we were there among the crowd of students, among the yellow-painted plywood mountains and craters, we could see our future selves in the close-cropped young men turning somersaults on the gymnastic turnstile and dousing themselves with the water captured and frozen by the camera as it fell from a large enamelled basin that was such a tender peach colour you immediately remembered your childhood, and somehow the colour made you trust the picture more and did more to make you want to go to Zaraisk to study than all the other photographs of aviation trainers that looked like the half-decayed corpses of aeroplanes teeming with tiny people.

Once the decision was made, the rest proved to be quite easy: Mitiok's parents, puzzled and scared by the way his brother had turned out, were glad that their younger son would have such a secure and reliable job. By this time my father was an inveterate drunkard who spent most of the time lying on the divan facing the wall, under a rug embroidered with a goggle-eyed deer: I don't think he even understood that I intended to be a flyer, while my aunt couldn't have cared less.

I remember the town of Zaraisk. Or rather, I can't really say I either remember it or I've forgotten it – there's so little in the place either to forget or remember. Right in the centre was a tall bell-tower of white stone, from which long ago some princess had leapt onto the stones below, and despite all the centuries that had passed, this incident was vaguely remembered by the townspeople. Next to the tower was the history museum, and not far from that were the post office and police station.

When we got out of the bus, a nasty slanting rain was falling, and it was cold. We huddled under a basement awning bearing the sign "Polling Station" and waited half an hour for the rain to pass over. Apparently they were drinking inside; a strong smell of onions and the sound of voices came from behind the door. Someone kept suggesting they should sing, and eventually elderly male and female voices were raised in song: "Let us rejoice while we're alive..."

The rain stopped, we went to look for the bus, and found the same one in which we'd arrived. It turned out we need not have got out, we could have waited in the bus while the driver was having his lunch. Small wooden houses began drifting past the windows, one after the other, then they stopped and the forest began. The Zaraisk Flying School was in the forest, well away from the town. It had to be reached by walking about five kilometres from the final bus stop, which was called 'Vegetable Shop' (there was no shop anywhere near, but we were told the name was left over from before the war). Mitiok and I got off the bus and set off along a road scattered with sodden ash keys; it led us deeper and deeper into the forest, and just when we were beginning to think we were going the wrong way we suddenly came up against gates made of welded metal pipes, decorated with large tin stars. On both sides the forest ran up to a tall fence of grey, unpainted planks with rusty barbed wire coiling along its top. We showed the sleepy soldier on gate duty our warrants from the district military enlistment office and the passports we had received only recently; we were admitted and told to go to the club, where a meeting was about to begin.

Immediately to the right of an asphalted roadway leading into the centre of a small settlement was the beginning of the Lunar Village I had seen in the magazine – it consisted of several long single-storey barracks buildings painted yellow, surrounded by a dozen or so tyres dug into the ground, and a special plot designed to look like a panoramic view of the surface of the Moon. We walked past it and came to the garrison club, where the boys who had come to enrol were crowded around the columns. Soon an officer came out, appointed someone sergeant, ordered us to register with the examination committee and then go and collect our kit.

The examination committee was sitting in a Chinese-looking lattice-work pavilion in the yard of the club – three officers drinking beer and listening to quiet Eastern music on the radio as they gave out numbered squares of cardboard in exchange for our papers. Then they led us over to the edge of a sports-field overgrown with grass that was waist-high (it was obvious no one had played any kind of sport on it for many years), and issued us with two army tents, which we were to live in during the exams. These were rolls of multi-layered rubber sheets that we had to stretch out over wooden poles set into the ground. We got to know each other as we dragged the beds into the tents and then set them up in two tiers – the bedsteads were old and heavy, with nickel-plated knobs that could be screwed on to their uprights if they weren't connected with another bed above them. They gave us these knobs separately, in a special bag, and when the exams were over, I secretly unscrewed one and put it away in the cigarette pack where I kept the plasticine pilot with the metal foil head, the only witness to that distant and unforgettable evening in the South.

We hardly seemed to spend any time at all in the tents, but when they were taken down, there was a dense growth of grass under the rubber groundsheets, colourless and repulsive, with thick stems.

I can hardly remember the actual exams. All I do remember is that they weren't difficult at all, and there was no chance to fill up the answer paper with all the formulae and graphs that had absorbed the long spring and summer days spent poring over the pages of textbooks. It was no problem for Mitiok and me to get a pass mark, and then came the interview, which scared everyone more than anything else. We were interviewed by a major, a colonel, and a little old man with a jagged scar on his forehead, dressed in worn overalls. I said I wanted to join the cosmonaut class, and the colonel asked me to define a Soviet cosmonaut. I thought for a long time, but I couldn't think of the right answer, and finally I realised from the examiners' bored expressions that they were about to send me out into the corridor.

"Alright," said the old man, who hadn't spoken a word before this, "do you remember how you first got the idea of becoming a cosmonaut?"

I was in despair, because I had no idea how to answer the question. It must have been despair that drove me to tell him about the red plasticine figure and the cardboard rocket that had no exit. The old man livened up straight away at this, and his eyes began gleaming. When I got to the part about Mitiok and me having to crawl along the corridor in gas masks, he even grabbed hold of my arm and laughed, which made the scar on his forehead turn bright crimson. Then he suddenly became serious.

"Do you realise how difficult it is to fly into space?" he asked. "And what if your Motherland requires you to lay down your life? What then, eh?"

"If it comes to it..." I said with a frown.

He stared me right in the eyes for maybe three minutes.

"I believe you," he said. "You can do it."

When he heard that Mitiok, who had wanted to fly to the Moon since he was a baby, was joining too, he noted down his name on a piece of paper. Mitiok told me afterwards that the old man spent a long time asking him why he particularly wanted to go to the Moon.

Next day after breakfast, lists of the successful applicants appeared on the columns of the garrison club: my name and Mitiok's were beside each other in the list, out of alphabetical order. Some of the boys trudged off to appeal, some of them jumped up and down for joy on the criss-crossed white lines of the asphalt, some ran to call home, and high above it all I recall the white streak of a vapour trail in the colourless August sky.

Those of us who were enrolled as first-year cadets were summoned to a meeting with the flight-training staff – the teachers were already waiting for us in the club. I remember heavy velvet drapes and a table across the full width of the stage, with officers sitting at it looking strict and official. The meeting was chaired by a youthful-looking lieutenant-colonel with a skinny pointed nose: while he was talking, I imagined him in flying-suit and pressurised helmet, sitting in the cabin of a MiG fighter covered in blotches, like expensive jeans.

"O.K. boys, we don't want to begin by talking about scary stuff, do we? But you know well enough we don't get to choose the times we live in – the times choose us. Maybe I shouldn't be giving you this kind of information, but I'm going to tell you anyway..."

The lieutenant-colonel paused for a second, bent down to

the major sitting beside him and whispered something in his ear. The major grimaced, rapped thoughtfully on the table with his pencil, and then nodded.

"Right," said the lieutenant-colonel in a quiet voice. "At a recent closed session of the political instructors of the armed forces, the times we are living in were defined as a Pre-War Period!"

The colonel paused, waiting for a response, but clearly the audience hadn't understood a thing – at least Mitiok and I hadn't.

"Let me explain," he went on, even more quietly. "The meeting was on July fifteenth, right? So up until July fifteenth we were living in a Post-War Period, but since then – a whole month already – we've been living in a Pre-War Period, is that clear or not?"

For a few seconds there was silence in the hall.

"I'm not saying this to scare you," the lieutenant-colonel went on, in a normal voice now, "but we have to remember the responsibility we bear on our shoulders, don't we? And make no mistake about it, by the time you get your diplomas and your ranks, you'll be Real Men with a great big capital M, the kind that only exist in the land of Soviets."

The lieutenant-colonel sat down, straightened his tie and touched the edge of a glass to his lips – his hands were shaking and I thought I could hear the faintest echo of his teeth rattling against the glass. The major stood up.

"Boys," he said in a melodious voice, "although it would be more correct now to call you cadets, but I'm just going to call you boys anyway. Boys! Remember the story of the legendary hero Alexei Maresiev, immortalised by Boris Polevoi in his book *The Story of a Real Man!* The hero our college is named after! He lost both legs in combat. But after losing his legs, he didn't lose heart, he rose up again on artificial legs and soared into the sky like Icarus to strike at the Nazi scum! Many people told him it was impossible, but he never forget what was most important – that he was a Soviet man! A Real Man! And you must never forget this, never, wherever you are! All of the flight-training staff and I personally, as assistant flight political instructor, promise that we will make Real Men of you in the shortest possible time!"

Then they showed us our places in the first-year cadets' barracks into which we were being moved from the tents, and took us to the mess-hall, where the dusty MiGs and ILs dangling on strings from the ceiling seemed like immense flying islands beside the squadrons of swift black flies.

The dinner was pretty bad: watery soup with macaroni stars, tough chicken with rice, and boiled fruit. After we'd eaten we felt really sleepy; Mitiok and I barely made it to our beds, and I fell asleep straight away.

5

The next morning I was woken by loud groans of pain and confusion right in my ear. In fact I'd been hearing the same sounds in my sleep for a long time, but I was only jerked into full wakefulness by a particularly loud and piteous wail. I opened my eyes and looked around. The surrounding beds were alive with a strange squirming and muffled bellowing – I tried to prop myself up on my elbow, but I couldn't, because I was bound to the bed with broad straps like the ones used to tie up suitcases that are stuffed too full: the most I could do was turn my head slightly from side to side. From the next bed I met the pain-filled eyes of Slava, a young village boy I had got to know the day before, and the lower part of his face was hidden by a tightly-tied piece of cloth. I tried to open my mouth to ask him what was wrong, but discovered that I couldn't move my tongue, and I had no feeling at all in the lower part of my face, as though it had gone numb. I guessed that my mouth must be bound and gagged too, but before I could feel surprised, I was struck by horror: where Slava's legs should have been, the blanket fell straight down in an abrupt step, and the freshly-starched blanket cover was stained with red blotches like the marks left on cotton towels by water-melon juice. What was even more terrifying – I couldn't feel my own legs and I couldn't lift my head to look at them!

"Platoon five!" the words thundered out in a sergeant's fruity bass, replete with an infinitude of allusions. "To the dressing station!"

About ten men immediately came into the ward – they were second- and third-year students (or more correctly, cadets in their second or third year of service, as I could tell from the stripes on their sleeves). I hadn't seen them before – the officers had said they were out helping with the potato harvest. They were wearing strange boots with tops that didn't bend, and they walked unsteadily, holding on to the walls or the ends of the beds. I noticed how pale and unhealthy their faces were, they seemed to bear the imprint of long days of interminable torment, to have been recast in a fixed expression of readiness. Inappropriately enough, at that moment I recalled the words of the Young Pioneers' greeting Mitiok and I had repeated with all the others on the distant parade square at summer camp – and I realised just what frauds we'd been, loudly assuring ourselves, our comrades in the line-up, and the transparent July morning that we were "always prepared".

The cadets wheeled the beds out into the corridor one after another, with the first-years bound down on them moaning and squirming, until only two were left in the room – mine and one by the window, on which Mitiok was lying. I couldn't get a proper look at him because of the straps, but I could see out of the corner of my eye that he was quiet and seemed to be asleep.

They came for us about ten minutes later, turned us round feet first, and wheeled us along the corridor. One cadet pushed the bed while another walked backwards and pulled it towards him; it looked like he was backing down the corridor and warding off the bed as it pursued him. We trundled into a long narrow lift with doors at both sides and went up, the second year student backed away from me down another corridor, and we stopped beside a door upholstered in black with a large brown plaque that I couldn't read because of my uncomfortable position. The door opened, and I was rolled into a room with an immense crystal chandelier in the shape of an aircraft bomb hanging from the ceiling, and the upper section of the walls decorated with a band of bas-relief ornamentation made up of sickles, hammers and urns entwined with grapevines.

They took my straps off, and I propped myself up on my elbows, trying not to look at my legs: straight ahead of me at the back of the room a green lamp stood on a massive desk that was illuminated by the slanting grey light from a tall narrow window. The person sitting at the desk was hidden from me by the open pages of a copy of *Pravda*, from the front of which a wrinkly face with radiantly kind eyes stared straight at me. The lino on the floor squeaked, and Mitiok's bed came to a halt beside mine.

The newspaper rustled a few times as its pages were turned, and then sank down onto the table.

There in front of us was the little old man with the scar on his forehead, the one who had grabbed me by the arm during the interview. Now he was wearing the uniform of a lieutenant-general with brocade at the button-holes, his hair was neatly brushed down, and his gaze was clear and sober. I noticed that his face seemed like a copy of the one that had been looking at me from the front page of *Pravda* just a minute before: it was just like in a film I saw where they showed one icon for a long time, and then another one gradually appeared in its place – the images were similar, but not quite the same, and because the transition was blurred, it seemed like the icon was changing in front of your eyes.

"Now boys, since you and I will be seeing quite a lot of each other for quite a long time, you can call me Comrade Flight Leader. Allow me to congratulate you on the results of your exams – and the interview in particular," said the old man, winking. "You have been registered immediately for the first year course at the KGB secret space training school – so you'll just have to wait a bit before you become Real Men. Meanwhile get ready to go to Moscow. I'll see you there."

I didn't realise what he'd said till we'd been taken back to the empty ward along those long corridors, where the lino sang a quiet song of nostalgia beneath the tiny castors of the bed, reminding me somehow of a day in July by the sea.

Mitiok and I slept the whole day (it seems they'd drugged our supper the previous evening – I was still sleepy the next day), and that evening a jolly yellow-haired lieutenant in squeaky boots came for us, and laughed and cracked jokes as he wheeled our beds out on to the asphalt parade-ground in front of platform with the concrete shell-shaped canopy, where several senior generals with kind intelligent faces, including Comrade Flight Leader, were sitting at a table. Of course, Mitiok and I could have walked there on our own, but the lieutenant said that this was standing orders for first-year cadets, and he ordered us to lie still so as not to upset the others.

All those beds stacked up against each other made the parade-ground look like the yard of an automobile factory or a tractor plant: a subdued groaning traced a complex flight path above it – dying away in one place, it sprang up in another, and then in a third, as though some huge invisible mosquito was darting about above the beds. On the way out the yellow-haired lieutenant told us that a combined graduation party and final state exam was about to begin.

Soon we were watching our lieutenant, the first of about fifty like him, as he danced the 'Kalinka' for the exam committee. He was pale and nervous, but he performed with incomparable mastery, to the sparse accompaniment of the assistant political instructor's accordion. The lieutenant was called Landratov – I heard his name when the Flight Leader handed him a red diploma and congratulated him on receiving it. Then the same dance was performed by all the others, and by the end I was bored stiff watching them. I turned to look at the sports field immediately beside the parade-ground – and suddenly realised why it lay under such a thick covering of wild grass.

I lay there and watched the stems swaying in the wind. The grey, rain-cracked fence topped with barbed wire just beyond the ruined soccer goal-posts seemed to me like the Great Wall, still stretching, despite all the warped and missing planks, all the way from the fields of distant China to the town of Zaraisk, making everything that appeared against its background look ancient and Chinese – the latticework pavilion where the exam committee worked, the obsolete fighter-plane, and the ancient army tents I could see from where I lay on my bed, clutching in my fist the nickel-plated knob I'd unscrewed for a souvenir.

The next day a truck carried Mitiok and me off through the summery woods and fields: we sat on our rucksacks, leaning against the cool steel of the side of the truck. I remember the edge of the tarpaulin swaying, and beyond it glimpses of tree-trunks and grey, dried-out telegraph poles from which the wires had long since been torn down. From time to time the trees parted and I glimpsed a pale, pensive triangle of sky. Then there was a halt and five minutes' silence, punctuated only by a dull, distant rattling; the driver, who had got out to relieve himself, explained that they were firing short bursts on the one or two machine guns they had at the shooting range close by. Then it was back to the truck's interminable jolting: I fell asleep, and woke up again for a few seconds only when we were already in Moscow, as the chink in the tarpaulin revealed a glimpse of a sight from some long-ago summer of my school-days – the archways of the shop 'Children's World' by the Lubyanka.

6

As a child I often used to imagine an open newspaper, still smelling of fresh ink, with a large portrait of myself right in the centre (wearing a helmet and a smile), and the caption: "Cosmonaut Omon Krivomazov feels just fine!" It's not easy to understand just why I wanted this so badly. Maybe I was dreaming of living part of my life through other people – the people who would look at this photograph and think about me, and try to imagine what I thought and felt, the inner workings of my soul. Most important of all, perhaps, I wanted to become one of these people myself – to stare at my own face, made up of thousands of typographic dots, and wonder what kind of films this man likes, and who his girlfriend is, and then suddenly remember that this Omon Krivomazov is me. Since then I've changed, gradually and imperceptibly. I've stopped being interested in other people's opinions since I realised that other people wouldn't be interested in me anyway, they wouldn't be thinking about me, but about my photograph, and with the same indifference I feel for other people's photographs. So the news that my heroism would remain unknown was no blow to me. The blow was the news that I would have to be a hero.

Mitiok and I were taken in by turns to see the Flight Leader the day after we arrived, as soon as we were kitted out in black uniforms, with bright yellow epaulettes bearing the incomprehensible initials 'HSS'. Mitiok went first, and I was called an hour and a half later.

When the tall oak doors first opened to admit me, I was astounded how closely the room resembled a scene from some war film. In the centre of the office stood a table covered with a big yellow map, with several men in uniform standing round it: the Flight Leader, three generals and two colonels, one a short fat man with a bright scarlet face, and the other a skinny man with thinning hair who looked like an aging sickly little boy – he was wearing dark glasses and sitting in a wheelchair.

"Commander of Central Flight Control Colonel Khalmuradov," said the Flight Leader, pointing at the fat man with the red face.

Khalmuradov nodded.

"Assistant Political Instructor of the Special Cosmonauts' Detachment Urchagin."

The colonel in the wheelchair turned his face towards me, leant forward in a slight bow and removed his glasses, as if to take a closer look at me. I couldn't help shuddering – he was blind; the lids of one eye had completely fused together, and whitish mucus gleamed dully between the lashes of the other.

"You may call me by my first name, Bamlag," he said in a high tenor voice. "I hope we're going to be friends, Omon."

The Flight Leader didn't introduce me to the generals, and nothing in their behaviour indicated that they even noticed I was there. I thought, though, that I'd seen one of them during the examinations at the Zaraisk Flying School.

"Cadet Krivomazov," said the Flight Leader, introducing me. "Well, shall we begin?"

He turned towards me, folded his hands on his belly and said:

"Omon, I'm sure you read newspapers and watch films, and you know that the Americans have landed some of their astronauts on the Moon and even driven around up there in a motor-carriage. Their goals are supposedly peaceful, but that all depends on how you look at things. Just imagine a simple working man from some small country, say in Central Africa..."

The Flight Leader wrinkled up his face and went through the motions of rolling up his sleeves and wiping the sweat from his brow.

"And then he sees that the Americans have landed on the Moon, while we... You understand?"

"Yes sir, Comrade Lieutenant-General!" I replied.

"The main purpose of the space experiment for which you will now be prepared, Omon, is to demonstrate that we do not lag behind the countries of the West in technology and that we are also capable of sending expeditions to the Moon. At the moment it is beyond our capability to send a piloted, recoverable ship. But there is another possibility – we can send an automated vessel, which will not have to be brought back."

The Flight Leader leaned over the protruding mountains and small hollow craters of the relief map. A bright red line cut across its centre, like a fresh scratch made with a nail.

"This is a sector of the lunar surface," said the Flight Leader. "As you know, Omon, our space science programme has mostly studied the far side of the Moon, whereas the Americans land on the bright side. This long line here is the Lenin Fissure, discovered a few years ago by one of our sputniks. Last year an automated expedition was sent to this unique geological formation to gather samples of the lunar surface, and the initial analyses have suggested that further investigation of the fissure is required. No doubt you know that our space programme is oriented mostly towards automation – it's the Americans who risk human lives. We only expose machines to danger. The idea is to send a special self-propelled vehicle, a so-called 'moonwalker', which will travel along the bottom of the fissure and transmit scientific information back to earth."

The Flight Leader opened the drawer of his desk and began rummaging about in it with his hand, keeping his eyes on me all the while.

"The overall length of the fissure is one hundred and fifty kilometres, but its width and depth are a matter of a mere few metres. It is proposed that the moonwalker will travel along it for seventy kilometres – the batteries should have enough power for that distance – and set up a radio-buoy at its centre-point, which will broadcast into space radio waves encoding the words 'Peace', 'Lenin' and 'USSR'."

A small, red toy appeared in his hand. He wound it up and set it at the beginning of the red line on the map. The toy began to buzz and edged forward – its fuselage was like a tin can set on eight small black wheels, with the letters 'USSR' on its side and two eye-like bulges at the front. Everyone followed its motion intently; even Colonel Urchagin turned his head in time with the others. The toy reached the edge of the table and tumbled onto the floor.

"Something like that," the Flight Leader said thoughtfully, casting a quick glance at me.

"Permission to speak, sir?" I heard my own voice.

"Fire ahead."

"Surely the moonwalker is automated, Comrade Lieutenant-General?"

"It is."

"Then what am I needed for?"

The Flight Leader lowered his head and sighed.

"Bamlag," he said, "your turn."

The wheelchair's electric motor hummed, and Colonel Urchagin moved away from the table.

"Let's go for a little walk," he said, driving over and taking hold of my sleeve.

I glanced enquiringly at the Flight Leader. He nodded. I followed Urchagin out into the corridor, and we began walking slowly along – that is, I walked and he rode beside me, adjusting his speed with a lever which was topped by a home-made plexiglass ball with a carved red rose inside it. Several times Urchagin opened his mouth and was about to speak, but each time he closed it again, and I was already sure he didn't know where to begin, when he suddenly grabbed my wrist in his narrow hand.

"Listen carefully now, Omon, and don't interrupt," he said with feeling, as though we'd just been singing songs together round the camp fire. "I'll start with the general background. You know, the fate of humanity is full of tangled knots, things that don't seem to make any sense, bitter realities hard to accept. You have to see things very clearly, very precisely, in order not to make too many mistakes. Nothing in history is like it is in the textbooks. Dialectics led to Marx's teaching, which was intended for an advanced country, but won its victory in the most backward one. We communists had no time to prove the correctness of our ideas – the war cost us too much of our strength, we had to spend too long struggling against the remnants of the past and our enemies within the country. We just didn't have the time to defeat the West technologically. But in the battle of ideas, you can't stop for a second. The paradox – another piece of dialectics – is that we support the truth with falsehood, because Marxism carries within itself an all-conquering truth, and the goal for which you will give your life is, in a formal sense, a deception. But the more consciously..."

I felt my heart sink, and I tried spontaneously to pull my wrist free, but Colonel Urchagin's fingers seemed to have turned into a narrow hoop of steel.

"... the more consciously you perform your feat of heroism, the greater will be the degree of its truth, the greater will be the meaning of your brief and beautiful life!"

"Give my life? What heroism?" I asked in a faint voice.

"Why, the very same heroism," he said equally quietly, sounding as though he was frightened, "that has already been demonstrated by more than a hundred young lads just like you and your friend."

He said nothing for a moment, and then continued in his former tone of voice:

"You heard it said that our space programme is based on automated technology?"

"Yes."

"Let's you and me go to room 329, and they'll tell you about our space automation techniques."

7

"Comrade Colonel!"

"Comrade Camel!" he echoed, mocking me. "They asked

you at Zaraisk if you were willing to give your life, didn't they? What answer did you give?"

I was sitting in an iron chair bolted to the floor in the centre of the room; my arms were clamped to the armrests, my legs to the chair's legs. The windows were covered with thick blinds, and in the corner there was a small writing desk with a telephone without a dial. Colonel Urchagin was sitting opposite me in his wheelchair; as he spoke he laughed, but I could tell he was deadly serious.

"Comrade Colonel, you must understand, I'm just an ordinary boy. You think I'm some kind of great... But I'm not one of those people who..."

Urchagin's wheelchair hummed as he began to move. He came right up close to me and stopped.

"Wait a moment, Omon," he said, "wait a moment. Now we're getting to the point. Just whose blood do you think the soil of this country of ours is watered with? Some kind of special blood, perhaps? From some kind of special people?"

He reached out a hand, felt my face and then struck me across the mouth with his dry little fist – not really hard, just hard enough for me to feel the taste of blood in my mouth.

"That's the kind of blood it's watered with. From lads like you..."

He patted me on the neck.

"Don't be angry," he said. "I'm your second father now. I can even take my belt to you. Why are you cringing like a woman?"

"I don't feel ready to be a hero," I answered, licking away the blood. "That is, I feel I'm definitely not ready... I'd rather go back to Zaraisk than..."

Urchagin leaned towards me and stroked my neck as he spoke in a soft and gentle voice:

"Don't be such a little fool, Ommy. You should know, my son, that that's what heroism is all about. No one's ever ready to be a hero – there's no way to prepare for it. Of course, you can practise till you're really good at running up to the gun-port and have the knack of falling neatly across it on your chest – we teach all of that. But you can't teach anyone the actual inner act of heroism, it can only be performed. The more you wanted to live before, the better for the act of heroic sacrifice. The country needs heroic feats, even invisible ones – they nourish that fundamental strength which..."

I heard a loud croaking sound. The black shadow of a bird flitted across the blinds, and the colonel fell silent. He pondered for a while in his wheelchair, then switched on the motor and trundled out into the corridor. The door slammed behind him and then opened again a moment later to admit a yellow-haired Air Force lieutenant carrying a length of rubber hose. His face looked familiar, but I couldn't figure out where I'd seen him before.

"Recognise me?" he asked.

I shook my head. He went over to the table and sat on it, his legs dangling down in their gleaming black boots with concertina folds, at the sight of which I remembered where I'd seen him – he was the lieutenant from the Zaraisk Flying School who had wheeled my bed and Mitiok's out on to the parade ground. I even remembered his name.

"Lan... Lan..."

"Landratov," he said, flexing the rubber hose. "I've been sent to have a talk with you. Urchagin sent me. You don't really want to go back to the Maresiev School, do you?"

"It's not that I want to go back there," I said. "I don't want to go to the Moon. To be a hero."

Landratov chuckled and slapped his hands on his belly and his thighs.

"Well now," he said, "so you don't want to? D'you think they'll leave you in peace now? Or just let you go? Or send you back to the School? And even if they do, have you got any idea what it's like when you get up from your bed and take your first steps on crutches? Or how it feels before the rain?"

"No," I said.

"Or maybe you think when your legs heal up it's a bed of roses? Last year two cadets were tried for state treason. From the fourth year they work on flight simulators – d'you know what those are?"

"No."

"Basically it's just like being in a plane, you sit in a cockpit with your control column and your pedals – only you're watching a television screen. So this pair of swine, instead of practising their Immelman loops, flew off west at minimal height and refused to respond to the radio. When they eventually dragged them out, they asked them what they thought they had been up to. Neither of them would say anything, but one answered the question later. Said he just wanted to feel what it was like, didn't he, just for a minute..."

"And what happened to him?"

Landratov smacked the rubber hose down on the table beside himself.

"What's it matter?" he said. "The main thing is, I can understand them. All that time you keep hoping that eventually you'll get around to flying, so when they finally tell you the truth... D'you think anyone needs you without legs? And the country's hardly got any planes, they just fly up and down the borders so the Americans can photograph them. And even then..."

Landratov fell silent.

"Even then?"

"Never mind. What I wanted to say was, d'you think that after Zaraisk you'd be hurtling through the clouds in a fighter plane? If you were lucky, you might just find yourself in a song and dance ensemble in some Airforce Defence district. But most likely you'd end up dancing the 'Kalinka' in some restaurant. A third of us take to drink and another third – the ones whose operation didn't go right – end up committing suicide. How d'you feel about suicide, anyway?"

"I don't really know," I said. "I never thought about it."

"Well I used to think about it. Especially during the second year, when they were showing tennis on the TV and I was on duty in the club with my crutches. I was real miserable. And then it passed. Once you can come to terms with yourself, it gets easier. So you just remember, if you get any thoughts like that, not to give in. You should be thinking about all the interesting things you'll see if you go to the moon. These buggers won't let you go alive, anyway. Better play along with them, okay?"

"You don't seem to like them much," I said.

"What's there to like them for? Every word they say is a lie.

Which reminds me, when you're with the Flight Leader, don't you mention anything about dying, or even about you flying to the Moon. Just talk about automatic systems, okay? Or we'll be having another little talk in this room. I follow orders."

Landratov swung his rubber hose through the air, then he took a pack of 'Flight' cigarettes from his pocket and lit up.

"That friend of yours agreed straight away," he informed me.

When I went out into the air, my head was spinning slightly. The inner yard, separated off from the city by the grey-brown blocks of the building, was very much like a part of a country village that had been cut out precisely to fit the yard and then transported here: there was a wooden summer-house with cracked and peeling paint, and a horizontal bar welded together out of iron pipes, with a strip of green hallway carpet hanging on it – someone must have been beating it and then forgotten it; there were allotments, a chicken-coop and a sportsfield, several table-tennis tables and a circle of old painted tyres half buried in the ground that immediately reminded me of photographs of Stonehenge. Mitiok was sitting on a bench by the exit: I went over and sat beside him, stretched out my legs and looked at the black uniform trousers tucked into my boots – after the conversation with Landratov I felt as though the legs in them weren't really mine.

"Is it all true?" Mitiok asked in a quiet voice.

I shrugged. I didn't know exactly what he meant.

"Alright, I can believe the stuff about the aeroplanes," he said. "But all that about the nuclear weapons... Maybe back in '47 you could still make two million political prisoners all jump at once. But we don't have them any more, and there are nuclear tests every month..."

The door I had just come out of opened, and Colonel Urchagin's wheelchair drove out; he braked and surveyed the yard several times with his ear. I realised he was looking for us in order to add something to what had already been said, but Mitiok stopped speaking, and Urchagin obviously decided not to bother us after all. The wheelchair's electric motor hummed and it moved away to the opposite wing of the building. As he rode past us, Urchagin turned his smiling face in our direction and the sunken hollows of his eye-sockets seemed to peer benevolently into our very souls.

8

I think most Muscovites know perfectly well what's going on deep below their feet during those hours when they're queuing at the 'Children's World' department store next to the KGB building or when they ride the metro through Lubyanka station, so I won't go over it all again. Let me simply say that the model of our rocket was full-size and there was room for another one just as big beside it. The lift was an old pre-war job that took so long to get down there that you could read two or three pages of a book on the way.

The model rocket was a rather patchy construction, with parts of it just knocked together from planks, and only the crew members' work-places were precise recreations of the real thing. It was all intended for practical training, which Mitiok and I would not begin for some time yet. Even so, we were moved straight into a spacious box down below, with two pictures pretending to be windows presenting a panoramic view of Moscow under construction.

There were seven beds, so Mitiok and I knew our numbers would soon be increased. The box was only three minutes' walk along a corridor from the training hall where the model rocket stood: an interesting thing seemed to happen to the lift – whereas before it had seemed to take a long time to go down, now it seemed to take even longer to go up.

We didn't go up very often, since we spent most of our free time in the training hall. Colonel Khalmuradov gave us a brief series of lectures on the theory of rocket flight, using the model rocket to illustrate his points. When we were studying the technical equipment, the rocket was simply a study aid, but when evening came and the main lights were turned off, sometimes, for a few seconds, the dim wall-lamps transformed it into something long forgotten and wonderful, a final greeting to Mitiok and me from our childhood.

He and I were the first to arrive. The other members of our crew appeared in the college over a period of time. The first was Sema Anikin, a short stocky village lad who had been a sailor. The black uniform really suited him – unlike Mitiok, who looked like a scarecrow in it. Sema was very calm and didn't speak much and spent all his time on training, as all of us should have done, although his job was the simplest and the least romantic. He was responsible for the rocket's first stage, and his young life, in the words of Urchagin, who loved pompous and convoluted phrases, was destined to be broken off a mere three minutes after take-off. The success of the entire expedition depended on the precision with which he performed his task, and if he made the slightest mistake, we would all face an early and senseless death. Sema obviously laboured under the burden of this responsibility, and he even trained in the empty barracks, honing his movements till they were completely automatic. He squatted down, closed his eyes and began moving his lips as he counted up to two hundred and forty, and then he began turning anticlockwise, performing complicated hand-movements every forty five degrees. Even though I knew he was mentally opening the catches that attached the first stage to the second, every time his movements reminded me of something out of a Hong Kong martial arts movie; having gone through this complex manual procedure eight times, he immediately fell on his back and kicked upwards powerfully with both legs, thrusting against the invisible second stage.

Our second stage was Ivan Grechka, who arrived about two months after Sema. He was a Ukrainian with light hair and blue eyes, who was transferred to us from the third year at Zaraisk, so he still walked with some difficulty. He had a certain kind of warm simplicity, as though he was always smiling at the world, and everyone he met loved him for this smile. Ivan became particularly close friends with Sema. They teased each other all the time and were constantly competing to see who was quicker and better at running through the operations to detach his stage. Sema was nimbler, but Ivan only had to open four catches, so sometimes he was quicker.

Our third stage, Otto Plucis, was a ruddy-faced meditative

Balt. As far as I can recall, he never once joined Ivan and Sema when they were practising in the barracks – he always seemed to be lying on his bunk doing the crosswords in *Red Warrior*, his legs in their painstakingly polished boots crossed on the gleaming nickel-plated bar of the bedstead. But you only had to see how he dealt with his share of the catches on the model to realise that if there was one reliable section in our rocket, then it was the separation system for the third stage. Otto was a funny guy. After the all-clear, he enjoyed telling stupid stories like the ones children tell to frighten each other at summer camp.

"Once this expedition flies off to the Moon," he would say in the darkness. "They've been flying for ages, and they're just getting close. Then suddenly the hatch opens and in come some people in white coats. The cosmonauts say: 'We're flying to the Moon!' The people in white coats say: 'Fine, fine. No need to get excited. We'll just give you this little injection...'"

Mitiok and I still hadn't begun technical equipment training when the training for the ballistics group was made more complicated. It hardly affected Sema Anikin – his feat of heroism took place at a height of four kilometres, and all he had to do was put on a padded workjacket over his uniform. It was harder for Ivan: at forty five kilometres, where his moment for immortality arrived, it was cold, and the air was already rarefied, so he trained in a sheepskin coat, tall fur boots and oxygen mask, which made it difficult for him to climb in through the narrow hatch on the model. Otto had things easier – a special space-suit was made for him, complete with electrical heating. It was sewn by the seamstresses at the Red Mountain clothing factory from several American high altitude suits captured in Vietnam, but it wasn't quite ready yet – they were still finishing off the heating system. In order not to lose time, Otto practised in a deep-sea diver's suit; I can still see his red, sweaty pockmarked face behind the glass of the helmet as it rose out of the hatch; when he said hello, the friendly words came out with strangely jumbled sounds.

The lectures on the general theory of automated cosmic systems were read to us in turn by the Flight Leader and Colonel Urchagin.

The Flight Leader was called Pkhadzer Vladlenovich Pidorenko. He got his name from the small Ukrainian village where he was born. His father had been in the Cheka too, and following the fashion of those days he'd taken his son's first name from the first letters of the Russian words for "Party and Economic Activists of the Dzerzhinsky District", while his second was an abbreviation of Vladimir Lenin: what's more, if you added up the letters in the two names Pkhadzer and Vladlen, there were fifteen, the same as the number of Soviet republics. But he couldn't stand being called by his own name, and subordinates who served with him called him either "Comrade Lieutenant-General" or, like myself and Mitiok, "Comrade Flight Leader". He pronounced the phrase "automated systems" with such pure, visionary intonation, that for a second his office in the Lubyanka, which we went up to for his lectures, was transformed into the sounding-board of some immense grand piano – but even though the phrase turned up in his speech quite often, he gave us absolutely no technical information, and spent most of the time telling us run-of-the-mill stories or reminiscing about his wartime days with the partisans in Belorussia.

Urchagin didn't deal with any technical topics, either. He usually nibbled on sunflower seeds, laughing as he spat out the shells, or told us jokes.

"How do you divide a fart into five parts?" he asked once.

When we said we didn't know, he answered himself:

"Fart into a glove."

And he would burst into thin laughter. I was amazed at the positive optimism of this man, blind, paralysed, chained to a wheelchair, but nonetheless carrying out his duty and never tiring of life. There were two political instructors in the space school who were very like each other – Urchagin and Burchagin, both colonels. It was Urchagin who usually taught our crew. There was only one Japanese wheelchair with an electric motor for the two of them, so when one of them was busy with educational work, the other would lie silent and motionless, propped up on his elbow on the bed in a tiny room on the fifth floor, wearing his uniform jacket and covered up to the waist with a blanket that hid the bed-pan from probing eyes. The poor furnishings of the room – a map-case for writing on, with narrow slits in the sheet of cardboard laid over it, a glass of strong tea permanently on the table, the white curtain and the rubber plant – it all touched me so profoundly I almost wept, and at those moments I stopped thinking that all communists were cunning, mean and self-serving.

The last member of the crew to arrive was Dima Matiushevich, who was responsible for the lunar module. He was very withdrawn, and despite his young years, quite grey. He kept himself to himself, and all I knew about him was that he'd served in the army. When he saw the reproduction of a painting by Kuindzhi that Mitiok had cut out of a magazine and hung over his bed, he hung a sheet of paper over his own bed, with a small drawing of a bird and three words in big block capitals: OVERHEAD THE ALBATROSS.

Dima's arrival coincided with the introduction of a new discipline into the timetable, known as 'Strong in Spirit'. It wasn't really a study subject in the normal sense of the word, although it was given pride of place on the timetable. We began to get visits from people who were professional heroes – all of them told us about their lives without a trace of sentimentality; their words were the same simple ones you heard in the kitchen at home, so the very essence of their heroism seemed to spring from the ordinary, from the petty details of everyday life, from the grey, cold air around us.

The person I remember best of all from these 'strong in spirit' is retired Major Ivan Trofimovich Popadya – a funny kind of name. He was tall, a real Russian Hercules, and his jacket was festooned with medals. His face and neck were red, and dotted all over with small white scars. He wore a patch over his left eye. His life was very unusual: he began as a simple huntsman in a hunting reserve used by Party leaders and members of the government, and his duties were to drive the animals – wild boar and bears – towards the marksmen hiding behind the trees. One day there was a terrible accident. A big male boar broke across the line of flags and fatally injured a Party leader who was firing from behind a birch tree. He died on the way to the nearby town, and a session of the supreme organs of power adopted a resolution forbidding the leadership to hunt wild animals. But, of course, the need remained, and one day Popadya was summoned to the Party Committee of the hunting reserve, where they explained the whole business to him and then said:

"Ivan! We can't order you to do it – and even if we could, we wouldn't, not this. But it's something that needs to be done. Think about it. We won't force you."

Popadya thought hard about it all night long, and next morning he went to the Party Committee and said he agreed.

"We didn't expect any other answer," said the Party Secretary.

They gave Ivan a bullet-proof waistcoat, a helmet and a boarskin, and he went to work at his new job – a job which it would be no exaggeration to describe as daily heroism. For the first few days he felt a little afraid, especially for his exposed legs, but then he got used to it, and the members of the government, who all knew what was going on, tried to aim at his side, at the bullet-proof waistcoat, which Ivan padded with a small pillow to soften the impact. Occasionally, of course, some old codger from the Central Committee would miss his aim, and then Ivan would go on extended sick-leave and read a lot of books, including his favourite, the memoirs of the famous flyer Pokryshkin. Just how dangerous this work was – every bit as bad as active military service – can be judged from the fact that every week they had to replace Ivan's bullet-riddled Party card, which he carried in the inside pocket of the boar skin. When he was wounded, his shift was worked by other huntsmen, including his own son Marat, but Ivan was always regarded as the most experienced, the one to be trusted with the most responsible jobs. They tried to take care of Ivan Popadya. Meanwhile, he and his son studied the habits and the calls of the wild inhabitants of the forest – the bears, wolves and boars – and improved their professional skills.

The accident happened a long time ago, when the American politician Kissinger visited our country. He was conducting important negotiations, and a lot depended on whether we could sign a provisional nuclear arms limitation treaty (this was especially important, because our enemies must not be allowed to know that we never had any nuclear arms). So Kissinger was entertained at the very highest state level, and all the various state services were involved – for instance, when it was discovered that he liked short, plump brunettes, a quartet of plump brunette swans was found to drift across Swan Lake on the stage of the Bolshoi Theatre, under the glinting gaze of Kissinger's horn-rimmed spectacles up in the government box.

It was thought easier to negotiate while hunting, and Kissinger was asked what he liked to hunt. Probably in an attempt at subtle political witticism, he said he preferred bears, and was surprised and rather alarmed when next morning he was actually taken hunting. On the way he was told that two Bruins had been lined up for him.

These two were none other than the communists, Ivan and Marat Popadya, father and son, the finest special-service huntsmen in the reserve. The guest of honour laid out Ivan straight away with a well-aimed shot, just as soon as he and Marat reared up on their hind legs and came out of the forest, roaring; they attached the hooks to the special loops on his body and dragged it over to the car. But the American just couldn't hit Marat, even at almost point-blank range, when Marat was deliberately moving as slowly as he could, exposing the full expanse of his chest to the American's bullets. Suddenly something quite unpredictable happened – the foreign guest's gun jammed, and before anyone realised what was happening, he had thrown it down in the snow and flung himself at Marat with a knife. Of course, a real bear would have dealt very quickly with any huntsman who behaved like that, but Marat remembered the responsibility he bore. He lifted up his paws and growled, hoping to frighten the American away, but the hunter was either drunk or crazy, and he ran up and stuck the knife into Marat's belly; the slim blade slipped between the plates of the bullet-proof vest. Marat fell. And all this happened as his father looked on from where he lay a few metres away; they dragged Marat over to him, and Ivan realised that his son was still alive – he was groaning almost inaudibly. The blood he left on the snow wasn't the special liquid from his little rubber bladder – it was the real thing!

"Hold on, son!" Ivan whispered, swallowing his tears. "Hold on!"

Kissinger was beside himself with delight. He suggested to the officials accompanying him that they should all drink a toast right there, standing on top of the "teddy-bears" as he called them, and they should sign the treaty on the spot. They covered Marat and Ivan with the board of honour from the wall of the forester's hut – it had their photographs on it – and made an improvised table. For the next hour, Ivan saw nothing but fleeting glimpses of feet, and he heard nothing but drunken speech in a foreign language and the swift muttering of the interpreter; he was almost crushed when the Americans danced on the table. When it grew dark and everybody left, the treaty was signed and Marat was dead. A thin trickle of blood flowed from his open jaws on to the blue evening snow, and a golden Hero of the Soviet Union star glittered on his fur, where the manager of the reserve had hung it. All night the father lay opposite his dead son, crying – and feeling no shame for his tears.

I suddenly understood anew the long-lost meaning of the words I was so fed up of seeing staring at me every morning from the wall of the training hall: "Life always has room for heroism." It was not just romantic nonsense, but a precise and sober statement of the fact that our Soviet life is not the ultimate instance of reality, but only, as it were, its ante-room. I imagined it this way: that there is no space anywhere in America, between the glaring shop window and the parked Cadillac, for heroism, and there can be no space for it – apart, of course, from that rare moment when a Soviet spy passes by. But here in Russia, you can only be on an apparently identical pavement outside an identical shop window in a Post-War or Pre-War Period, and this is what opens the door leading to heroism, not in the external world, but within, in the very depths of the soul.

"Well done," said Urchagin, when I shared my thoughts with him, "only, be careful. The door leading to heroism certainly does open up within us, but it is in the external world that the act of heroism takes place. Don't fall into subjective idealism, or your proud flight aloft will be robbed in a single short second of all its meaning."

9

It was May, the peat bogs around Moscow were on fire, and a pale sultry sun hung in the smoke-veiled sky. Urchagin gave me a book to read, by a Japanese author who had been a kamikaze pilot during the Second World War, and I was astounded by the similarity between my state and the feelings he described. Just like him, I didn't think about what lay ahead of me, but lived for the present day – engrossing myself in books and leaving the world completely behind as I gazed at the fiery explosions on the cinema screen (on Saturday evenings they showed us war films), even worrying seriously about my marks, which weren't too good. The word "death" existed in my life like a note reminding me of something I had to do that had been hanging on my wall for ages – I knew it was still there, but I never paused to look at it. Mitiok and I never discussed the subject, but when we were finally told it was time for us to begin practising on the actual space equipment, we glanced at each other and seemed to feel the first breath of an icy wind.

From the outside the moonwalker looked like a large laundry tank set on eight heavy tram wheels. Numerous differ-ent items protruded from its fuselage – various-shaped anten-nae, mechanical arms and so forth. None of these worked, and they were really only there for television, but they were very impressive all the same. The lid of the moonwalker was covered with small oblique incisions: this was not deliberate, it was simply that the metal sheeting it was made from was the same as they used on the floor in the metro, but then again, it made the machine appear more mysterious.

The human psyche works in peculiar ways: it needs details first of all. I remember when I was small I often used to draw tanks and aeroplanes and show them to my friends, and they always liked the drawings with lots of lines that didn't really mean anything, so I actually began adding them on purpose. In just the same way, the moonwalker managed to look like a very complicated and ingenious piece of equipment.

The lid hinged up to one side – it was hermetically sealed with rubber padding and had several layers of thermal insulation. Inside, in a space about the same size as the turret of a tank, there was a slightly modified sports bike frame, with the pedals and just two gearwheels, one of which was neatly welded to the axle of the rear pair of wheels. The handlebars were ordinary semi-racers – they could just turn the front wheels slightly via a special transmission system, but I was told the necessity shouldn't arise. Shelves, empty for the time being, protruded from the walls; attached to the centre of the handlebars was a compass, and attached to the floor was the green tin box of a radio transmitter with a telephone receiver. Set in the wall in front of the handlebars were the black spots of two tiny round lenses, like the spy-holes in apartment doors; through them I could see the edges of the front wheels and a decorative mechanical arm. On the opposite wall hung the radio speaker, a perfectly ordinary square block of red plastic with a black volume control: the Flight Leader explained that in order to counter the sense of psychological isolation from the native land, all Soviet space vehicles received programmes broadcast from Moscow's Beacon radio station. The large, convex external lenses were covered by blinkers above and at the sides, so that the moonwalker had something like a face, a crude and likeable face, like the faces they draw on melons and robots in children's magazines.

When I first climbed inside and the lid clicked shut over my head, I thought I would never be able to stand being cooped up and cramped like that. I had to hang over the bicycle frame, distributing my weight between my hands on the handlebars, my legs braced against the pedals, and the saddle, which didn't really support part of my weight so much as determine the position my body had to adopt. A cyclist bends over like that when he's trying to get moving really fast – but at least he can straighten up if he wants to, whereas I couldn't, because my back and my head were practically jammed against the lid. But then, after about two weeks of practice, when I began to get used to it, it turned out there was quite enough space in there to forget about feeling cramped for hours at a time.

The round spy-hole lenses were immediately in front of my face, but the lenses distorted everything so badly there was no way I could tell what was there outside the thin steel wall of the hull. A small spot of the ground just in front of the wheels and a ribbed antenna were powerfully magnified in clear focus, but everything else was dissolved into zig-zags and blobs, as though I was gazing down a long dark corridor through tears on the glass lenses of a gas-mask.

The machine was fairly heavy, and it was hard to get it moving – I even began to doubt whether I would be able to power it across seventy kilometres of lunar desert. Just one turn round the yard was enough to make me really tired; my back ached and my shoulders hurt.

Every other day now, taking turns with Mitiok, I went up in the lift, then out into the yard, stripped down to my vest and underpants, climbed into the moonwalker and strengthened the muscles on my legs by riding round and round the yard, scattering the chickens and occasionally running over one of them – not deliberately, of course, it was just that through the lenses there was no way to tell a huddled chicken from a newspaper, for instance, or a leg-wrapping the wind had blown off the clothes-line, and I couldn't brake fast enough, anyway. At first Urchagin drove in front of me in his wheelchair to show me the way – through the lenses he was a blurred grey-green blob – but gradually I got the hang of it, so I could drive round the entire yard with my eyes closed. All I had to do was set the handle bars at a certain angle, and the machine went round in a smooth circle, coming back to its starting point. Sometimes I even stopped looking through the spy-holes and just let my muscles work away, putting my head down and thinking my own thoughts. Sometimes I remembered my child-hood, sometimes I used to imagine what the rapid approach of the final moment before eternity would feel like. And sometimes I tried to finish off really old thoughts that resur-faced into consciousness. For instance, I thought about the question "Who am I?"

It was a question I often used to ask myself as a child, when I woke early in the morning and stared up at the ceiling. Later on, when I was a bit older, I began to ask it in school, but the only answer I got was that consciousness is a property of highly organised matter, according to Lenin's theory of reflection. I didn't understand what these words meant, and I remained as astonished as ever. How was it that I could see? Who was this "I" who saw? And what did it mean, to see? Did I see anything outside me, or was I simply looking at myself? And what did that mean – outside myself and inside myself? I often felt like I was on the very threshold of the answer, but when I tried to take the final step, I suddenly lost sight of the "I" that was about to cross the threshold.

When my aunt went out to work, she often asked an old neighbour to look after me, and I used to ask her the same questions, taking real pleasure in seeing how hard it was for her to answer them.

"Inside you, Ommy, you've got a soul," she said, "and it looks out through your eyes, but it lives in your body like your hamster lives in that saucepan. And this soul is a part of God, who created all of us. And you are that soul."

"But then why did God stick me in this saucepan?" I asked.

"I don't know," said the old woman.

"And where is he?"

"Everywhere," said the old woman, gesturing with her arms.

"Then that means I'm God too?" I asked.

"No," she said. "Man isn't God. But he's made in God's image."

"And is Soviet man made in God's image too?" I asked, stumbling over the unfamiliar phrase.

"Of course," said the old woman.

"Are there many gods?" I asked.

"No. There is only one."

"Then why does it say in the handbook that there are lots of them?" I asked, nodding towards the atheist's handbook standing on my aunt's bookshelf.

"I don't know."

"Which god is best?"

The old woman gave the same answer again:

"I don't know."

Then I asked:

"Can I choose for myself, then?"

"You choose, Ommy," the old woman laughed, and I began rifling through the handbook, which had heaps of different gods in it. I especially liked Ra, the god the ancient Egyptians believed in thousands of years ago. Probably I liked him because he had a falcon's head, and pilots and cosmonauts and all sorts of heroes were often called falcons. I decided that if I really was made in a god's image, then it should be this one. I remember taking a large exercise book and copying the following extract into it:

"In the morning Ra, illuminating the Earth, sails along the heavenly Nile on the barque Manjet, in the evening he transfers to the barque Mesektet and descends into the underworld, where he does battle with the forces of darkness as he sails along the nether Nile, and in the morning he reappears on the horizon."

In ancient times, people could not know that the Earth really circles the Sun, said the dictionary, and so they invented this poetic myth.

Under the article in the dictionary was an old Egyptian picture showing Ra transferring from one barque to the other: two identical boats were drawn up side by side, and a girl in one was handing a girl in the other a hoop with a falcon sitting in it – that was Ra. What I liked most of all was that in among all the weird and wonderful items in the boats there were four grim five-storey houses which looked just like the ones built in the Moscow suburbs in Khruschev's time.

From then on, although I responded to the name 'Omon', I always thought of myself as 'Ra': that was the name of the hero of the imaginary adventures I had before I fell asleep, when I closed my eyes and turned to face the wall – until the time when my dreams were affected by the usual developmental changes.

I wonder if anyone who sees a photograph of the moonwalker in the newspapers will imagine that inside this steel saucepan, which exists for the sole purpose of crawling seventy kilometres across the Moon and then halting for eternity, there is a human being, gazing out through two glass lenses? But what does it matter? Even if someone guesses the truth, he'll never know that this human being was me, Omon Ra, the faithful falcon of the Motherland, as the Flight Leader once called me, putting his arm round my shoulder and pointing through the window at a brightly glowing cloud.

10

Another subject that appeared in our study timetable – 'The General Theory of the Moon' – was classed as optional for everyone except Mitiok and me. The classes were given by a retired Lieutenant Colonel of Philosophy, Ivan Evseievich Kondratiev. Somehow I didn't take to him, although I had no real reason for disliking him, and his lectures were quite interesting. I remember the unusual way he began his first class with us – he spent half an hour reading out various poems about the Moon from pieces of paper; eventually he became so moved that he had to stop and wipe off his glasses. I still used to take notes then, and what I was left with from this class was a senseless accumulation of fragmentary quotations: "Like a golden drop of honey sweetly gleams the Moon... Of the Moon and hope and quiet glory... The Moon, how rich the meaning of this word for every Russian ear... But the world has other regions, oppressed by the tormenting Moon, to highest strength and supreme courage forever out of reach... But in the sky, schooled to endure all things, a senselessly distorted disc... He did control the flow of thought, but only by the Moon... The cheerless liquid Moonness..." And so on for another page and a half. Then Lieutenant Colonel Kondratiev grew more serious and began speaking in an official sing-song voice:

"Dear friends! Let us recall the historical words of Vladimir Ilyich Lenin, written in 1918 in a letter to Inessa Armand. 'Of all the planets and heavenly bodies,' Lenin wrote, 'the most important for us is the Moon.' Many years have passed since then, and the world has changed in many ways, but Lenin's assessment has lost none of its acuteness and fundamental relevance: time has confirmed its correctness, and the fire of these words of Lenin's still illuminates today's page in the calendar. Indeed, the Moon plays an immense role in the life of humanity. The famous Russian scientist Georgy Ivanovich Gurdjiev developed the Marxist theory of the Moon during the early illegal period of his activity. According to this theory, the Earth had five moons in all – this is in fact why the star which is the symbol of our state has five points. The fall of each of the moons has been accompanied by social upheavals and catastrophes – thus, the fourth moon, which fell to earth in 1904, and is known as the Tungus Meteorite, provoked the first Russian revolution, which was soon followed by the second. Previous moon-falls led to changes in sociopolitical formations – of course, the cosmic catastrophes did not affect the level of development of the forces of production, which is determined independently of human will and consciousness, or the emanations of the planets, but they did facilitate the development of the subjective preconditions for revolution. The fall of our present moon – the fifth and final one – will usher in the absolute victory of communism throughout the solar system. On this course we shall study Lenin's two major works on the Moon – 'The Moon and Rebellion' and 'Advice from an Outsider'. We'll begin today with a review of bourgeois falsifications of the question – those views which assert that organic life on earth serves merely as nourishment for the Moon, as the source of emanations which it absorbs. This is incorrect, for the goal of the existence of organic life on earth is not to feed the Moon, but, as Lenin demonstrated, to build a new society, free from exploitation of men numbers one, two and three by men numbers four, five, six and seven..."

And so on. He said a lot of other complicated things, but what I remember most vividly is an image that struck me as amazingly poetical: a weight hanging on a chain makes a clock work. The Moon is such a weight, the Earth is the clock, and life is the ticking of the gears and the singing of the mechanical cuckoo.

We had fairly frequent medical check-ups – they studied every one of us inside and out, which was understandable. So when I heard that Mitiok and I had to have what they called a "reincarnation check", I thought they would just be testing our reflexes or measuring our blood pressure. I didn't know what the first word meant.

But when I was summoned downstairs and I saw the specialist who was going to examine me, I felt an uncontrollable childish fear, which was quite out of place in view of what the immediate future held in store for me.

The person facing me was not a doctor with a stethoscope sticking out of the pocket of his white coat, he was an officer, a colonel – only he wasn't wearing a uniform jacket, he was dressed in a strange black robe with epaulettes. He was large and fat, with a red face that looked as though it had been scalded with hot soup. Hanging on a string round his neck were a whistle and a stop-watch, and if not for his eyes, which were like the observation slit of a heavy tank, he would have looked like a football referee. But anyway, he was pleasant enough and laughed a lot, and by the end of the conversation I felt relaxed. He spoke with me in a small office where there was nothing but a table, two chairs, a couch covered with imitation leather and a door leading into another room. He filled up several yellowish forms, gave me a measuring-glass of some bitter liquid to drink and set a small hour-glass on the table. Then he went out through the second door, telling me to follow him when all the sand had fallen through the hour-glass.

I remember watching the hour-glass and being amazed at how slowly the grains of sand tumbled down through the narrow glass neck, until I realised that it was because each grain had its own will, and none of them wanted to fall, because for them that was the same as dying. And at the same time they had no choice, it was inevitable. The next world and this one are just like this hour-glass, I thought: when everyone alive has died in one direction, reality is inverted and they come to life again, that is, they begin to die in the opposite direction.

This made me feel sad for a while, and then I noticed that the grains of sand had stopped falling a long time ago, and I ought to go and join the colonel. I felt agitated, and at the same time strangely light and airy; I remember taking ages to walk to the door behind which he was waiting for me, although in fact it was only two or three steps away. I reached for the handle and pushed, but the door didn't open. Then I tried pulling it towards me, and suddenly noticed that I wasn't pulling at a door, but a blanket. I was lying in my bed, and Mitiok was sitting on the edge. I felt dizzy.

"Well? What was it like in there?" asked Mitiok. He looked oddly excited.

"What? Where?" I asked, raising myself up on one elbow and trying to think what had happened.

"At the reincarnation check," said Mitiok.

"Hang on," I said, remembering how I'd just been pulling on a door handle, "hang on... No. I don't remember a thing."

I felt strangely empty and lonely, as though I'd been walking through fields in autumn for a long time. This was such an unusual feeling that I forgot everything else, including even the sense of approaching death that had been constantly with me during the last few months: it was no longer so sharp now, it was simply there as the background for all my other thoughts.

"Did you sign a promise not to tell?" Mitiok asked scornfully.

"Leave me alone," I said, turning to face the wall.

"These two fat-faced warrant officers in black robes just dragged you in here," he went on, "and they said to me 'Here, take back your Egyptian'. And your blouse is covered in puke. Can't you remember anything at all?"

"Not a thing," I answered.

"Well, wish me luck," he said. "I have to go now."

"Break a leg," I said. All I wanted to do was to sleep, because it seemed to me that if I fell asleep quickly enough, I'd wake up as myself again.

I heard Mitiok close the squeaky door behind him, and then it was morning.

"Krivomazov! The Flight Leader wants you!" one of our group yelled in my ear. I didn't really wake up until after I was already dressed. Mitiok's bed was empty and undisturbed: the other guys were sitting on their beds in just their vests. I could feel the tension in the air as they glanced awkwardly at each other, and Ivan wasn't even cracking any of those stupid, but very funny, morning jokes of his. Something had happened, and all the way up to the Flight Leader's office on the third floor above ground I tried to figure out what it was. As I walked along with my eyes screwed up against the sunlight that pierced through the curtains – I was so unused to it – I noticed my reflection in a huge dusty mirror standing in a bend in the corridor, and I was amazed at how deathly pale my face was. I realised that my feat of heroism had really begun a long time ago.

The Flight Leader stood up to greet me and shook my hand.

"How's the training going?" he asked.

"Fine, Comrade Flight Leader," I said.

He looked into my eyes, checking me out.

"Yes, I can see it is. The reason I sent for you, Omon, is that I want you to help me. Take this tape-recorder," he said, pointing to a small Japanese cassette-player on the table in front of him, "and these forms and a pen, and go to room number 329. It's free just at the moment. Have you ever transcribed a tape recording?"

"No," I replied.

"It's easy. You play a bit of the tape, write down what you heard, and then play a bit more. If you can't make it out the first time, you listen to it as often as you need to."

"I understand. Permission to go?"

"Granted. No, wait. I think you'll understand why I'm asking you to do this for me. Very soon you'll have all sorts of questions that no one down there will answer," as he spoke, the Flight Leader jabbed his finger towards the floor. "I could have decided not to answer them too, but I think it's better for you to know what's going on. I don't want you tormenting yourself unnecessarily. But bear in mind that neither the political instructors nor the crew must know what you find out. What's happening now is a breach of discipline on my part. So you see, even generals commit them sometimes."

Without speaking, I picked up the tape-recorder from the table, together with a few yellow forms – they were the same as the ones I had seen the day before – and went to room 329. The curtains on the windows were firmly closed, and the metal chair with the leather straps on the legs and arm-rests still stood in the middle of the floor, only now there were wires leading to it from the wall. I sat at a small writing desk in the corner, placed a ruled sheet of paper in front of me, and switched on the tape-recorder.

"Thank you, Comrade Colonel... It's very comfortable, more like an armchair, really, ha-ha-ha... Of course I'm nervous. It's kind of like an examination, isn't it?.. I understand. Yes. Two 'i's – Sviridenko..."

I switched off the tape-recorder. It was Mitiok's voice, but it was strange somehow, as though someone had attached a blacksmith's bellows to his vocal chords instead of his lungs – he was speaking in a relaxed, sing-song fashion, always on the out-breath. I wound the tape back a bit and pressed 'Play'. I didn't stop the tape again after that.

"... like an examination, isn't it?.. I understand. Yes. Two 'i's – Sviridenko... No thanks, I don't smoke. No one in our group does, they wouldn't fit in... Yes, over a year now. I can hardly believe it. As a kid I used to dream of flying to the Moon... Of course, of course. That's right, only people with hearts as pure as crystal. They have to be, with all the Earth spread out below... About who on the Moon? No, I've never heard anything about it... Ha-ha-ha, you're pulling my leg... But your room is a bit strange – well, unusual. Is it like this everywhere here, or just in this special section? All those skulls on the shelves, my God – lined up just like books. And all with labels, look... no, I didn't mean that. If they're on the shelves, there must be a reason. Autopsies, some kind of archives... I understand. I understand. Really, now!.. How on earth was it saved?.. And this here, over the eye, is that from the ice-pick?.. Mine. There were two more forms as well. The final check is just before blast off. Yes. I'm ready. But Comrade Colonel, I gave all the details... Just talk about myself, since I was a child? No, thank you, I'm quite comfortable... Well, if that's the procedure. You should have headrests, like they have in cars. The pillow could fall down if I lean forward... Aha, I was just wondering why you have that mirror on the wall. So you stand the other one on the table. What a thick candle... Made of what? Ha-ha-ha, you're joking, Comrade Colonel... That's incredible. Honestly, it's the first time I've seen anything like it. I read about it somewhere, but I've never seen it done. Incredible. It's like a corridor. Where? Into this one? Holy Jesus, what a lot of mirrors you have, it's like being in a hairdresser's. Why no, what do you mean, Comrade Colonel?.. It's just a turn of phrase I picked up from my grandmother. I'm a scientific atheist, otherwise I wouldn't have gone to the aviation college... I remember fairly well. I didn't move to Moscow till I was eleven – I was born in one of those small towns on a railway line – a train goes by once in three days, and nothing else happens. Absolutely nothing. The streets are filthy, and the geese walk down the middle. Lots of drunks. Everything is grey – winter, summer, it makes no difference. Two factories, a cinema. And the park, of course, but it's better not to stick your nose in there. And then, you know, when there's this buzzing in the sky, you lift up your eyes and watch. No need to explain that... And I was always reading books, I owe everything that's good in me to them. My favourite, of course, was 'The Andromeda Nebula', that really made an impression on me. Just imagine it – an iron star... And on this planet black as night – a Soviet star ship, with a swimming pool, in the middle of a circle of blue light, and where the light ends – a hostile life-form that fears the light and has to stay hidden in the darkness. Some kind of medusas or other – I didn't really understand what they were – and there's this black cross – I think that's a hint at the church and the priests. This black cross creeps through the darkness, and the people are working where the blue light is, mining anameson. And then the black cross zaps them with some weird energy! It aimed for Erg Noor, but Niza Krit shielded him with her breast. Afterwards our guys took their revenge – a nuclear strike out to the horizon. They saved Niza Krit and they caught the boss medusas and packed them off to Moscow. And I was thinking while I read it, what great work they do in our embassies abroad! It's a good book. I remember another one, too... There was this cave..."

"..."

"No, the cave came later, and it wasn't a cave, it was

corridors. Low corridors with ceilings covered in soot from torches. At night the warriors carried torches while they guarded the Lord Prince. Protecting him from the Akkadians, so they said. Actually from his brother, of course... Forgive me Lord Commander of the North Tower, if I say what I shouldn't, but everyone here thinks the same – all the warriors and the servants. And even if you order my tongue to be cut out, anyone will tell you the same thing. It was Queen Shubad herself who garrisoned the troops here, as protection against Meskalamdug. Whenever he goes hunting he always rides along the southern wall, with two hundred warriors in pointed bronze caps – why does he need them to hunt lions? Everyone talks about it. Of course not, Lord Commander of the North Tower, you must have been chewing cinquefoil again! I'm Ninhursag, priest of Arrata and carver of seals. That is, when I grow up, I shall be a priest and a carver, I'm still a boy as yet... What's that you're writing? Why, you know me. You gave me that bridle with the bronze pendants. Don't you remember? Why... Just a moment... I was sitting with Namtura – you know him, his ears were cut off – and he was teaching me how to carve a triangle. That was the hardest shape of all for me. First you make two deep cuts, and then you use a broad chisel to prise it out from the third side and... Yes, that's right, and then someone outside dragged open the curtain insolently and we looked up, and there were two warriors standing there. Great joy! they said. Our prince is a prince no longer, but the great king Abaraggi! He had just departed to the deity Nanna, and so we also had to make ready to leave. Namtura wept from happiness, he began singing something in Akkadian and tying his things together in a bundle. But I went straight out into the yard, telling Namtura to gather up the chisels. By Urshu the mighty! The warriors carrying torches made the yard as bright as day! Why no, Lord Commander of the North Tower, of course not. Namtura mumbles away like that all the time... No, I never offered any sacrifices, either. Don't. I am now the Nuun of the great king Abaraggi, it is not such a simple matter to have my ears cut off, you need a royal decree... Very well, I forgive you. Then the Lord Master of the Bolt came up to me and said: Ninhursag, take this dagger of state bronze, you are a man now. And he gave me a bag of barley flour – you will prepare your food along the way, he said. Then I looked, and saw them walking around the yard in their bronze caps. Great Urshu! I thought. I mean, Great Anu! Meskalamdug and Abaraggi must have made peace... But then, how can you argue with a king when his every word is Anu. Then they showed me my chariot and I climbed up into it. There was another boy standing in it – he drove the bulls. I'd never seen him before. All I remember is that he had beads of turquoise, expensive beads. And a dagger in his belt – he'd just been given one too. When I looked round at the fortress I felt a bit sad. But then the clouds parted, and the Moon shone so brightly through the gap... And I felt so relaxed and happy... Then they moved aside the stone slab in the cliff wall beside the stables, and there was the entrance to the cave. I never knew there was a cave there. I really didn't... May I never be valorous in battle! It was you there! I remember now. And then, Lord Commander of the North Tower, you came over to us with two bowls of beer and said it was from the king's brother Meskalamdug. You were wearing the same skirt, but you had a painted bronze cap on your head. We drank it down. I'd never drunk beer before. Then the other boy shouted something, and tugged on the reins, and we set off – straight into the gap in the cliff-face. I remember the road led downwards, and along the sides – I couldn't see, it was dark... Afterwards? Afterwards I found myself here in your tower. Was it the beer that affected me like that?.. Will they punish me? Intercede for me, Lord Commander of the North Tower. Tell them what happened. Or give them the tablets – you've written it all down. Of course I have it... No I won't give you it, I'll apply it myself. No one gives away their own seal, by U... Anu the Intercessor! There! Do you really like it? I made it myself. It took three attempts to get it right. This is the god Marduk. What fence? Those are the higher gods. Intercede for me, Lord Commander of the North Tower! I'll carve three seals for you. No, I'm not crying... There, I've stopped. Thank you. You are a man of wisdom and power. Don't tell anyone I was crying... They'll say, what kind of priest of Aratta is he, if a drink of beer makes him cry... Of course I want to. Where?

To the South or the North? Your wall is entirely covered in mirrors. I understand... Yes, I know that. It was when Ninlil went to bathe in the clear flowing waters, and then came out on to the bank of the canal. Her mother told her again and again, but still she came out on to the bank of the canal, and Enlil put a child in her belly there. And afterwards he came to Kiur and the council of the gods said: Enlil, violator of women, be gone from the city! And of course, Ninlil followed him... No, it's not too bright. The other two? That was later, when Enlil disguised himself as a watchman at the ford and Ninlil was already carrying Nanna beneath her heart..."

" ..."

"But then, those two are simply different aspects of one and the same deity. You could say that Hecate is the dark and mysterious aspect, while Selene is the bright and marvellous aspect. But I must admit I'm not very knowledgeable in this area – I just heard a thing or two in Athens... Yes, I was. In Domitian's time. I was hiding there. Otherwise, Father Senator, you and I wouldn't be riding in this sedan-chair now... The usual thing – *lèse majesté*. They claimed my master had a statue of the Princeps in his courtyard, and two slaves were buried beside it. He never had such a statue. Even under Nerva we were afraid to go back. But there's nothing to be afraid of with the present Princeps. He sent Plinius Secundus himself to us as his Legate – how the times have changed, glory be to Isis and Serapis! It's no accident... Why no, what do you mean, Father Senator, I swear by Hercules! I picked that up in Athens, the place is just packed with Egyptians... What interesting tablets you have, you can hardly see the wax at all. And the lion's muzzles – are they electron? You don't say, Corinthian bronze... It's the first time I've seen it.... But you already know me – Sextius Rufinus. No, I'm a freedman. A sedan-chair is really a marvellous thing – if the slaves are skilful, that is – you can write as you ride along. And the lamp burns just like in a room, and the stone-pines float past outside... Well now, Father Senator, I see you can read a man's heart. I'm constantly composing verse to myself. It's not Martial, of course, I'm just blunting styli really... 'I sing a song in petty verse, As one time Catullus did sing, And also Calvus and the ancients. What does

it matter to me? I have chosen verse, quitting the forum...' I
exaggerate, of course, Father Senator, but that's what poetry is
for. Actually, it was literature that made me a witness in the
trial of the Christians. I went to see our Legate. A great man...
Well, I wasn't exactly a witness. No, no, I wrote down everything just the way it was – he really is from Galilee, that
Maximus. They meet at his house by night and breathe some
kind of smoke. Then he goes up on the roof wearing nothing
but his sandals and crows like a cock – as soon as I saw it I
knew they were Christians... I made up the bit about the bats,
of course. But what does it matter? They're bound for the
gladiator school anyway. But I really took a liking to our
Legate. Yes... He invited me over to his table and read my
verse. Then he said: Sextius, you must come to dinner. At the
full moon. I'll send someone for you, he said. I gathered up all
my scrolls of verse – he's bound to send them to Rome, I
thought. I put on my finest cloak... No, I can't wear the toga,
I'm not a Roman citizen. We set off, but the road led out of
town. We were travelling a long time, and I fell asleep in the
carriage. When I woke up I saw a building, something between
a villa and a shrine, and torch-bearers. Well, we went inside
and through into the courtyard. There was a table already laid
under the open sky, and everything was lit up by the Moon – it
was unbelievably huge. The slaves said to me, the Lord Legate
will be out in a minute, lie down at the table and have some
wine. This is your place, under the marble lamb. I lay down
and began to drink, and all the others lying there kept looking
at me in silence. I wonder, I thought, what the Legate can have
told them about my verse... I began to feel quite uncomfortable. But then two harps began to play behind a screen, and
suddenly I felt so happy – it was remarkable. Somehow I found
myself up on my feet and dancing... And then tripods of fire
appeared, and some other people in yellow tunics. I think they
were a little out of their minds – they just sat there and sat
there, then suddenly they would stretch out their arms towards
the Moon and start singing something in Greek... No, I
couldn't make it out – I was dancing and enjoying myself. Then
the Lord Legate appeared – he was wearing a pointed Phrygian
cap with a silver disc and carrying a reed-pipe. His eyes were

glittering. He poured me more wine. You write fine verse, Sextius, he said. Then he started talking about the Moon – exactly like you, Father Senator. Heh, heh, I keep wondering what we're doing riding in this sedan-chair? That's right... You're in your toga now, but then you were wearing a tunic and a pointed Phrygian cap, like the Legate's. Yes, and you were holding a red lance with a horse's tail. I felt awkward about turning my back to you, but the Legate kept saying to me, look at Hecate, Sextius, and I'll play my pipe for you. He started playing – really quietly, and I looked up and went on looking, and then you started asking me about Hecate and Selene. But how did I manage to get into your sedan-chair? Is anything wrong? Well, praised be Is... Hercules. Apollo and Hercules... Very well, I'll take them back, I brought them for the Legate to read. Are you a literary man too, Father Senator? I see you keep writing all the time. Aha. A keepsake. You liked the verses too. 'This hour for you does Liei walk, and in her hair – a regal fragrant rose.' Of course. Let me apply my cameo. Never mind, the carving is quite shallow, it doesn't need much wax to print the image. Are we almost there? Thank you, Father Senator, my hair was rather dishevelled. How much would a mirror like that cost in the metropolis? You don't say? In Bythinia we can buy a house for that sum. Is it Corinthian bronze too? Silver? And there's an inscription..."

" ..."

"Never mind, I can make it out. Now... 'To Lieutenant Wulf for Eastern Prussia. General Ludendorf.' Oh, I beg your pardon, Brigadenführer, it came open by itself. What a remarkable cigar case, it shines just like a mirror. So in nineteen fifteen you were already a lieutenant? And a flyer too? Come now, Brigadenführer, it's embarrassing. Because of these three crosses I can't fly a single assignment. There are plenty of Yaks and MiGs, they say, but we only have one Vögel von Richthofen. If it weren't for this special mission, I'd probably be mouldering in an empty barracks somewhere... Yes, my name is written just like 'bird'. My mother was upset at first, when she found out what my father wanted to call me. But then Baldur von Schirach – he was a friend of my father's – dedicated an entire poem to me. They study it in the schools nowadays... Careful, they're shooting from that window over there... Oh, no, the wall's good and thick... I can imagine what he would have written if he'd known about the special mission. It was a real poem all in itself. I believed them when they said they were transferring me to the Western Front, and I only found out what was happening in Berlin. At first, of course, I was annoyed. Have they nothing better to do in Anenerbe, I thought, than to recall combat pilots from the front? But when I saw the plane – Holy Virgin Mary! Straight away... Why, of course not, Brigadenführer, it's just that I lived in Italy as a child. Yes. In all my years of flying I never saw anything so beautiful. It took some time for me to work out what it actually was – an Me-109 with a special engine and extended wings... Damn, the magazine's jammed... Okay, I'll fix it... Anyway, the moment I stepped into the hangar it took my breath away. So light and white – it seemed to glow in the darkness. But what really surprised me was the training. I thought I'd be studying equipment, but instead of that they used to bring me to you at Anenerbe and measure my skull, and all the time Wagner's music was playing. If I asked any questions, no one answered. When they woke me up that night, I was sure they were going to measure my skull again. But no, when I looked out of the window there were two Mercedes standing there with their engines running... Excellent shot, Brigadenführer! Right on the turret. Where on earth did you get the knack... Well, we got in and drove away. Afterwards... Yes, there was a cordon of SS men with torches. We drove past them and came out of the forest, and there was a building with columns, and an airfield. There was no one at all around, just a light breeze blowing and the Moon in the sky. I was sure I knew all the airfields around Berlin, but I'd never seen this one. My plane was standing there on the runway, with something white hanging under the fuselage, like a bomb, but they would not even let me stop beside it, they brought me straight into this building... No, I don't remember. All I remember is the Wagner. They told me to get undressed and they washed me like a child... No, let's keep the grenades, we'll need them later... So they massaged my skin with oil – it smelt of something ancient, a pleasant kind of smell. And they gave me a flying suit, entirely white. With all my decorations on the chest. Well, Vögel, I thought, this is it... All my life I dreamed of something of the sort. Then the men from Anenerbe said: walk across to the plane, captain. They'll tell you everything there. They all took turns to shake me by the hand, and I set out. My boots were white too, I was afraid to step in the dust ... Just a moment... I went up to the plane, and there... Why, it was you, Brigadenführer, not in that helmet, but in a black pointed cap... And you started explaining everything to me – ascent to eleven thousand, set course for the Moon and press the red button on the left panel... Damn. Just missed one!... They gave me a white map-case, and then coffee with cognac from a thermos flask. No thank you, I said, I don't drink before take-off, and you said strictly: do you know who sent that coffee, Vögel? Then I turned round and I saw him – I would never have believed it. Just like in the newsreels, even the same double-breasted jacket. But he was wearing a pointed cap and there was a pair of binoculars round his neck. And the moustache was a bit wider than it is in the portraits... Or perhaps the moonlight made it look like that. He waved, just like in the stadium... So anyway, I drank the coffee, got into the plane, put on the oxygen mask and took off. And immediately I felt so good, my lungs felt huge. I climbed to eleven thousand and set a course for the Moon – it was immense, it seemed to cover half the sky – and I looked down. Everything below looked green, and there was a river glinting... Then I pressed the button, and I began keeling over to the right, and I can't remember how I made a landing... Sign it? And you scribble something down for me as a keepsake. Thank you... Did many of them break through to Berlin? That's clear enough... It's nothing, from the crushed brick, probably. My nose isn't broken... Aha, I see, it's nothing at all. You could shave with a cigar-case like this, and you wouldn't need a mirror... Thank you..."

"..."

"No thank you, no more. I didn't really ask for it. You put them there yourself, Comrade Colonel, when you lit the candle... Well, what next – I read a lot of books, and then I made myself a small telescope. I looked at the Moon mostly.

Once I even got dressed up as a moonwalker for one of the school shows. I remember that evening very well... All the kids were gathered in the hall in their simple costumes – they could all dance. But in my costume, if I went down on all fours, I looked just like a moonwalker. The hall was filled with music, everyone was getting red in the face... I stood by the door and then crawled around the empty school on all fours. The corridors were dark and empty. I crawled up to a window, and outside up in the sky was the Moon. It wasn't even yellow, but kind of green, like in Kuindzhi's picture – do you know it? I have it hanging above my bed, I cut it out. It was then I swore to myself I would get to the Moon... Ha-ha-ha... If you do your best for me, Comrade Colonel, then I'm sure to get there... What next? After school I went to the Zaraisk Flying School, and then straight here... Does that give you some idea? Yes, I know, Comrade Colonel, it's always better man to man... Sign it? You don't mind blue ink? That's right. A simple heart, a short statement... Yes, please. Raspberry, if possible. Where do you get the cylinders for the syphon? Oh, what a silly question... Comrade Colonel, may I ask another question? Is it true they bring the soil from the Moon to your department? I don't remember, someone in our crew... Of course I would like to see it, I've only seen it on television... What! How much does a jar like that hold, about three hundred grammes? Could I? Thank you... Thank you very much... Could you give me another sheet, just to pack it better... Thank you. I remember. To the right along the corridor to the lifts, and then down. I won't make it? It's still affecting me? Alright then, show me... What a strange pointed cap you have. No, I like it. We had caps like that in the army during the civil war. Very handsome, but unusual, no peak and a round cockade... No, I haven't forgotten. Left, you say? And why are you carrying that torch? The electrician... I see, he needs a special pass. Light the way for me, the steps are steep... just like in our landing module. Comrade Colonel, it's a dead end..."

There was a click, and then the different sound of a man and woman singing in unison. The brightness in their voices contrasted jarringly with what I had been listening to.

I turned off the tape-recorder – I felt terribly afraid.

I remembered the colonel in the black robe with the whistle and the stop-watch hanging round his neck, and I realised that no one had asked Mitiok any questions – every time he had responded to the quiet note of the whistle, as it interrupted his monologue.

11

None of the others asked me about Mitiok. He wasn't actually friendly with anyone except me, apart from playing a few games with home-made cards with Otto. His bed was already gone from our box, and only the coloured pictures from the magazines were left hanging on the wall to remind us that a boy called Mitiok had ever existed. In class everyone acted as though nothing had happened; Colonel Urchagin was particularly cheery and jolly.

Meanwhile our small group, which seemed not to notice the loss of one of its members, carried on as usual. No one actually said as much, but it was obvious: we would be flying soon. The Flight Leader met with us several times to tell us how he fought in a partisan detachment during the war; we had our photographs taken – first separately, then all together, and then in front of the banner with all the teaching staff. Above ground we began to run into new cadets – they were being trained separately from us, and I didn't actually know what for: there was talk of sending some automatic probe to Alpha Microcephalus immediately after our expedition, but I was never really certain that the new boys were the probe's crew.

One evening in early September I was unexpectedly summoned to the Flight Leader. He wasn't in his office, and the adjutant in the ante-room, who was trying to combat his boredom with an old number of *Newsweek*, told me he was in room 329.

I could hear voices and something that sounded like laughter behind the door with the number '329'. I knocked, but no one answered. I knocked again and turned the handle.

A cloud of tobacco smoke hovered just below the ceiling, reminding me somehow of that vapour trail in the airspace over the Zaraisk Flying School. There was a small Japanese

man sitting in the metal chair in the centre of the room, his
arms and legs strapped down – I knew he was Japanese from
the white rectangle with a round red sun on the sleeve of his
flying suit. His lips were blue and swollen, one eye was shrunk
to a narrow slit in the centre of a crimson bruise, and his
overalls were spattered with blood – some of the red spots were
fresh, others were already dried and brownish-looking.
Landratov was standing in front of the chair in his tall gleaming boots, wearing the dress uniform of a lieutenant of the Air
Defence Forces. Over by the window a short young man in
civilian clothes was leaning against the wall with his arms
crossed on his chest. The Flight Leader was sitting at the table
in the corner, staring absentmindedly right through the
Japanese and tapping on the table with the blunt end of a
pencil.

"Comrade Flight Leader!" I began, but he stopped me with
a wave of his hand and began gathering into a file the papers
that were scattered about the table. I looked across at
Landratov.

"Hi," he said, extending a broad palm in my direction,
then, taking me completely by surprise, he punched the
Japanese right in the stomach. The Japanese croaked faintly.

"The bastard doesn't want to go on a joint mission!"
Landratov said, and shrugged, his eyes round with astonishment; then he turned his feet out in an unnatural fashion and
performed a quick dancing squat with a double slap to his
boots.

"Stop it, Landratov!" barked the Flight Leader, getting up
from the table.

I heard a low whine, filled with hatred, coming from the
corner of the room, and when I looked I saw a dog sitting up
on its hind legs in front of a dark-blue bowl with a picture of a
rocket on it. It was a very old husky, with eyes that were
completely red, but more astonishing to me than its eyes was
the light-green uniform jacket that covered its body, with the
epaulettes of a major-general and two orders of Lenin on the
chest.

"Let me introduce you," said the Flight Leader, catching
my eye. "Comrade Laika. The first Soviet cosmonaut. Her

parents, by the way, were colleagues of ours. They worked in the security branch, too, but up in the North."

A small flask of brandy appeared in the Flight Leader's hands, and he poured some into the bowl. Laika made a feeble snap at his wrist, but missed, and then she began whining again.

"She's a smart one," the Flight Leader said with a smile. "If only she wouldn't piss all over the place. Landratov, go and get a rag."

Landratov went out.

"*Ioi o tenki ni narimasita ne,*" said the Japanese, parting his lips with some difficulty. "*Hana va sakuragi, hito va fudzi-vara.*"

The Flight Leader turned an inquiring expression to the young man by the window.

"He's delirious, Comrade Lieutenant-General," said the young man.

The Flight Leader picked up his file from the table.

"Let's go, Omon."

We went out into the corridor and he put his arm round my shoulders. Landratov passed us with a rag in his hand, and as he closed the door of room 329 he winked at me.

"Landratov's still young," the Flight Leader said thoughtfully. "He's a bit wild. But he's a fine flyer. Born to it."

We walked on a few metres in silence.

"Well now, Omon," said the Flight Leader, "you're for Baikonur the day after tomorrow. This is it."

I'd been expecting the words for months, but still it felt like I'd been hit in the solar plexus by a snowball with a heavy metal bolt inside it.

"Your call-sign, as you requested, is 'Ra'. It was hard," the Flight Leader gestured upward significantly with his finger, "but we won out in the end. Only don't you say anything yet down there." He jabbed his finger downwards.

During the final test run on the model rocket I was simply a spectator – the other guys did the test while I sat on a bench by the wall and watched. I had passed my test a week earlier, up in the yard, when I rode the fully-equipped moonwalker round a figure of eight a hundred metres long in six minutes. The team's timing was spot on, and afterwards we were lined up in front of the rocket for a farewell photograph. I never saw it, but I can easily imagine what it looks like: at the front is Sema Anikin in his padded jacket, with streaks of engine-oil on his hands and face; behind him, leaning on an aluminium cane is Ivan Grechko in his long sheepskin coat, with an oxygen mask dangling on his chest; behind him, in a silver spacesuit padded with warm patches of flannelette blanket decorated with yellow ducklings, is Otto Plucis – his helmet was pushed up and back, making it look like a hood frozen solid in the cosmic frost. Next is Dima Matiushevich, in a space suit that's exactly the same, except the blanket has plain green stripes instead of ducklings; the last member of the team is me, in my cadet uniform. Behind me, in his electric-powered chair, sits Colonel Urchagin, with the Flight Leader standing to his left.

"And now, following established tradition for these occasions," the Flight Leader said when the photo had been taken, "we'll go up and spend a few minutes on Red Square."

We walked across the hall, and lingered for a moment by the small iron door – lingered for a final look at the rocket that was an exact replica of the one on which we would soon go soaring up into the sky. The Flight Leader took a key from the bunch he carried and opened a small iron door in the wall, and we set off along a corridor which led in a direction that was new to me.

We wove this way and that for quite a while between stone walls festooned with wires of various colours: the corridor made several turns, and at times the ceiling was so low that we had to stoop. In one place I noticed faded flowers lying in a shallow niche, and on the wall beside it was a small memorial plaque with the words: "On this spot in 1932 Comrade Serob Nalbandian was villainously slain with a spade." Then a red carpet-runner appeared under our feet, the corridor began to widen out and finally ended at a staircase.

The staircase was very long, and it was flanked by a smooth incline a metre wide with narrow steps at its centre. I realised why it was built that way when I saw the Flight Leader pushing Colonel Urchagin's wheelchair up it. When he tired,

Urchagin put on the hand brake and they stood still for a while, so the others didn't walk too fast, especially since long flights of steps were difficult for Ivan to cope with. Eventually we arrived at a pair of heavy oak doors covered with carved emblems; the Flight Leader unlocked the doors with another of his keys, but they were swollen from damp and only opened when I put my shoulder against them and shoved with all my strength.

The daylight was dazzling: some of us put a hand over our eyes, others turned away, and only Colonel Urchagin sat there calmly, with the usual half-smile on his face. When we got used to the light, it turned out we were facing the grey headstones in front of the Kremlin wall, and I guessed we must have come out of the back entrance of the Lenin Mausoleum. It was so long since I'd seen the sky over my head that I felt dizzy.

"Every single one of our Soviet cosmonauts," the Flight Leader said softly, "has come here before their flight, to these stones that are sacred to every Soviet citizen, in order to take a little part of this place into space with them. Our country's labours have been hard and long, it all began with nothing but gun-carts and machine guns, and now you young lads work with highly complex automatic systems," he paused and ran a cold, unblinking gaze round all our eyes, "which have been entrusted to you by the Motherland, and which Bamlag Ivanovich and I have explained to you in our lectures. I am sure that as you tread the surface of the Motherland for the final time you will each take with you a little part of Red Square, though just what that particle will be for each of you, I cannot say..."

We stood in silence on the surface of our native planet. It was daytime. The sky was slightly overcast, and the sweeping branches of the blue firs swayed gently in the wind. There was a scent of flowers. The bells began chiming five o'clock: the Flight Leader glanced at his watch, adjusted the hands, and said that we still had a few minutes.

We went out on to the steps in front of the main door of the Mausoleum. There was no one at all on Red Square, unless you counted the two sentries who had just come on duty and gave no sign at all that they saw us, and three sentries' backs receding in the direction of the Spasskaya Tower. I glanced around, drinking in everything I saw and felt: the grey walls of GUM, the hollow fruit and vegetable shapes of St. Basil's Cathedral, the Lenin Mausoleum, the green dome topped by a red flag that I knew was behind the wall, the pediment of the Historical Museum, and the low grey sky, which looked as though it had turned its back on the Earth, and was probably still unaware that soon it would be ripped open by the iron phallus of a Soviet rocket.

"It's time," said the Flight Leader.

The guys walked slowly back behind the Mausoleum. A minute or so later only Colonel Urchagin and I were left under the word 'LENIN'. The Flight Leader looked at his watch and coughed, but Urchagin said:

"One moment, Comrade Lieutenant-General. I want to say a few words to Omon."

The Flight Leader nodded and withdrew around the polished marble corner.

"Come here, my boy," said the colonel. I went over to him. The first large, scattered raindrops were falling on the cobble-stones of Red Square. Urchagin groped in the air, and I held out my hand to him. He caught it, squeezed it slightly and tugged it towards him. I bent over, and he began to whisper in my ear. As I listened to him I watched the steps in front of his wheelchair gradually turning darker in the rain.

Comrade Urchagin spoke to me for about two minutes, pausing at length between his words. When he stopped talking, he squeezed my hand again and let go of it.

"Now go and join the others," he said.

I took a step in the direction of the Mausoleum, then turned back and asked:

"What about you?"

The raindrops were falling more and more thickly.

"No matter," he said, extracting an umbrella from a holster-like case on the side of the wheelchair. "I'll ride around here for a while."

And that was what I carried away with me from Red Square that early evening: the darkened cobblestones and a thin figure in an old military jacket, sitting in an invalid chair and struggling to open a black umbrella.

Dinner was pretty bad that evening: soup with macaroni stars, skinny chicken with rice and boiled fruit; usually when I'd drunk the liquid, I ate all the boiled fruit, but this time after I'd eaten a single bitter wrinkled pear, I began to feel sick and I pushed my plate away.

12

It felt like I was riding on a pedal-boat through thick reeds with huge telegraph poles sticking up out of them. The pedal-boat was strange somehow, unusual, the pedals not in front of the seat, but improvised from an ordinary bicycle: set between the two thick, long floats was a bicycle frame with the word 'Sport' on it. I hadn't any idea where all these reeds and the pedal-boat had come from, or what I was doing there. But I wasn't really bothered about it. Everything around me was so beautiful I just wanted to ride on and on and keep looking, and probably I'd have been quite happy to go on like that for ages. The sky was particularly lovely – long, narrow, lilac-coloured clouds hung above the horizon, looking like a string of strategic bombers. It was warm; I could just hear the propeller splashing in the water, and there was an echo of distant thunder from the west.

Then I realised it wasn't thunder. At regular intervals everything in me – or everything around me – was shaken, and my head began to buzz. With every successive blow all my surroundings – the river, the reeds, the sky over my head – seemed to fade a little more. The world was becoming as familiar in its finest details as the door of the toilet at home seen from the inside, and it was all happening very quickly, until I noticed that the bicycle was no longer on water or surrounded by reeds, but inside a transparent sphere that separated me off from everything around me. Every blow made the wall of the sphere thicker and more solid; it let through less and less light, until finally there was total darkness. Then the sky over my head was replaced by a ceiling, a feeble glow of electric light appeared, and the walls began to change their shape, closing in on me and bending out to form shelves stacked with glasses, cans and other stuff. And then the rhythmical shuddering of the world became what it had been from the very start – a telephone ringing.

I was sitting on the saddle inside the moonwalker, clutching the handlebars and leaning right down over the frame; I was dressed in a padded jacket, a fur cap with ear-flaps and fur boots; an oxygen mask hung round my neck like a scarf. The ringing came from the green box of the radio screwed to the floor. I picked up the receiver.

"Why, you fucking useless shithead!" a monstrous bass voice boomed in my ear in a tone of anguished suffering. "What're you doing in there, wanking?"

"Who's that?"

"Head of Central Flight Control Colonel Khalmuradov. Are you awake?"

"What?"

"Fuck you, that's what. Make ready, one minute to launch!"

"Ready in one minute, sir!" I muttered in reply, biting my lip in horror and grasping for the wheel with my free hand.

"You ass-hole," the receiver hissed indistinctly and began croaking – the man yelling at me was obviously holding the receiver away from his face while he talked to someone else. Then there was a ping in the phone, and I heard a different voice, mechanical and impersonal, but with a strong Ukrainian accent:

"Fifty-nine... fifty-ate..."

I was in that state of shame and shock that makes a man groan out loud or scream obscenities; the thought that I'd almost made an irrevocable mistake obscured everything else. As I followed the numbers exploding in my ears, I tried to remember what had happened and realised I probably hadn't really done anything all that terrible. All I could remember was lowering the glass of boiled fruit from my mouth and getting up from the table after I suddenly lost my appetite. The next thing I knew, the phone was ringing and I had to answer it.

"Tirty-tree..."

I noticed the moonwalker was fully equipped. The shelves that had always been empty before were densely stacked – on the bottom shelf there were tins of 'Great Wall' Chinese corn beef, covered in gleaming vaseline, on the upper shelf there was a map-case, a mug, a tin-opener and a pistol in a holster, everything secured by wire. Resting against my left hip was an oxygen cylinder with the word "Inflammable" on it, and against my right hip an aluminium milk-churn that reflected the light of the small electric lamp glowing on the wall. Under the lamp hung a map of the Moon marked with two black circles: under the lower circle were written the words "Landing Site". Hanging beside the map on a piece of string was a red marker pen.

"Sax-teen..."

Beyond the two spy-holes there was total darkness – which was what I should have expected, I realised, since the moonwalker was covered by the rocket's nose-cone.

"Nine... Ate..."

I recalled Comrade Urchagin's words: "Those final seconds of the count-down, what are they but the voice of history speaking through millions of television screens?"

"Tree... Two... Win... Blastoff."

Somewhere far below me I heard a rumbling and roaring that grew louder with every second until soon it was beyond all imagining, as though hundreds of sledge-hammers were pounding on the rocket's iron fuselage. Then the shuddering began, and I banged my head against the wall in front of me a few times – if not for the fur cap, I'd probably have beaten my brains out. A few tins of corn beef fell to the floor, then everything suddenly keeled over so sharply I thought for a second we were going to crash – and the next moment there was a distant voice in the telephone receiver that I was still pressing to my ear:

"Omon! You're flying!"

"We're off," I remembered my instructions and yelled, just like Gagarin did when he was first catapulted out into space.

The roaring became a steady, powerful rumbling, while the shuddering became the kind of vibration you feel in a train when it's already picked up speed. I put the receiver back on the hook, and the phone immediately rang again.

"Omon, are you alright?"

It was Sema Anikin's voice, speaking over a monotonous recitation of information about the first section of the flight.

"I'm fine," I said. "But why are we... Ah, I see..."

"We thought they'd have to postpone the launch, you were so sound asleep. The moment's calculated to the split second. The entire trajectory depends on it. They even sent a soldier up the gantry and he kicked the nose-cone to wake you up. They were trying to call you on the radio for ages."

"Aha."

We said nothing for a few seconds.

"Listen," Sema began again, "I've only got four minutes left, not even that. Then I have to detach the first stage. We've all said goodbye to each other, except for you... This is our last chance to talk."

I couldn't think of the right words to say, and all I felt was embarrassment and weariness.

"Omon!" Sema called me again.

"Yes, Sema, " I said, "I hear you. We're flying, d'you understand?"

"Yes," he said.

"How are you feeling?" I asked, realising just how senseless and insulting the question was.

"I'm okay. How about you?"

"Me too. What can you see?"

"Nothing. There's no way to see out. The noise is terrible. And the shaking."

"Up here too," I said, then stopped.

"Okay," said Sema, "my time's up. You know what? Think about me when you land on the Moon, okay?"

"Of course," I said.

"Just remember there was a guy called Sema. The first stage. Promise?"

"I promise."

"You've got to get there and finish the job, you hear me?"

"Yes."

"Time's up. Goodbye."

"Goodbye, Sema."

There were several hollow knocks in the receiver, and then through the crackle of interference I heard Sema's voice loud and clear as he sang his favourite song.

"O-oh, in Africa there's a river as long as this... O-oh, in Africa there's a mountain as high as this... O-oh, crocodiles and hippos... O-oh, monkeys and rhinos... O-oh... Ah-ah-ah-ah..."

On the word "rhinos" there was a crackling like a piece of tarpaulin ripping, and a moment later there was just short beeps, but just a second before that – if it wasn't my imagination – Sema's song turned into a scream. I was jolted again, my back hit against the ceiling and I dropped the receiver. From the change in the roaring of the engines, I guessed the second stage had begun firing. Probably the most terrible thing for Sema was switching on the engine. I imagined what it was like – breaking the safety glass and pressing the red button, knowing all the while that a second later the huge gaping openings of the rocket-tubes would spring into violent life. Then I remembered Ivan, and I grabbed the receiver again, but it was still beeping. I hit the hook a few times and yelled:

"Ivan! Ivan! Can you hear me?"

"What is it?" I finally heard him say.

"Sema, he's..."

"Yes," he said, "I heard it all."

"Are you going soon?"

"In seven minutes," he said. "D'you know what I'm thinking about now?"

"What?"

"I suddenly remembered how I used to catch pigeons as a kid. You know, we took this big wooden crate and sprinkled breadcrumbs under it and stood it on edge, and we propped up the opposite edge with a stick with about ten metres of string tied to it. Then we hid in the bushes or behind a bench, and when a pigeon wandered under the crate, we pulled the string. Then the crate fell on it."

"That's right," I said. "We did the same."

"And you remember, when the crate comes down, the pigeon starts trying to fly off and beats its wings against the sides, so the crate even jumps about?"

"I remember," I said.

Ivan didn't say anything else.

In the meantime it had turned quite cold. And it was harder to breathe, too – after every movement I wanted to catch my breath, as if I'd just run up a long flight of stairs. I began lifting the oxygen mask to my face to take a breath.

"And I remember how we used to make bombs with cartridge-cases and the sulphur from matches. You stuff it in real tight, and there has to be a little hole in the side, and you put several matches in a row beside it..."

"Cosmonaut Grechka," the bass voice in the receiver was the one that had woken me with abuse before the start of the flight. "Make ready."

"Yes, sir," Ivan answered without enthusiasm. "And then you tie them on with thread – insulating tape's better, because sometimes the thread comes loose. If you want to throw it out of the window, say from the seventh floor, so it explodes in mid-air, then you need four matches. And..."

"Stop that talking," said the bass voice. "Put on your oxygen mask."

"Yes, sir. You don't strike the last one with the box, though, the best thing is to light it with a dog-end. Or else you might shift them away from the hole."

I heard nothing after that except the usual crackle of inter-ference. Then I was bounced against the wall again, and the short beeps sounded in the receiver. The third stage had fired. The fact that my friend Ivan had just departed this life at an altitude of forty-five kilometres – as simply and unpretentiously as he did everything – strangely failed to make any impression on me. I didn't feel any grief; quite the opposite, I felt a strange exhilaration and euphoria.

I suddenly realised that I was losing consciousness. That is, I didn't notice when I lost consciousness, I noticed when I regained it. A moment ago I was holding the receiver to my ear, and now it was lying on the floor; there was a ringing in my ears, and I gazed down at it in stupefaction from my saddle up under the ceiling. A moment ago the oxygen mask was hanging round my neck like a scarf – and now as I shook my head in an effort to rouse myself, it was lying on the floor beside the telephone receiver. I realised I needed oxygen, so I reached for the mask and put it to my mouth – I felt better instantly, and I could feel I was very cold. Fastening all the buttons of my padded jacket, I put the collar up and lowered the ear-flaps of my fur-cap. The rocket was shaking slightly. I wanted to sleep, and even though I knew it wasn't a good idea, I couldn't fight it – I folded my hands on the handlebars and closed my eyes.

I dreamed of the Moon – the way Mitiok used to draw it in our childhood: a black sky, pale yellow craters and a distant mountain range. Walking slowly and smoothly towards the blazing orb of the sun hanging above the horizon was a bear, with its front paws held out in front of its muzzle: it had the golden star of a Hero of the Soviet Union on its chest and a trickle of dried blood ran from the corner of its mouth, which was set in a pitiful grin. Suddenly it stopped and turned its face towards me. I felt it watching me, and I raised my head to glance into its motionless blue eyes.

"I, and this entire world, are nothing but a thought someone is thinking," the bear said in a quiet voice.

I woke up. Everything was very quiet. Clearly some part of my consciousness had maintained contact with the outside world, and the sudden silence had affected me like an alarm clock going off. I leaned down to the spy-holes in the wall. The nose-cone had already separated from the rocket, and there in front of my eyes was the Earth.

I tried to work out how long I'd been asleep, but I couldn't put any definite figure on it. It must have been a few hours at least: I felt hungry already, and I began rummaging through the things on the upper shelf – I thought I saw a can-opener there, but it wasn't there now. I decided it must have been shaken off onto the floor, and started looking around for it, but just at that moment the phone rang.

"Hello!"

"Stand by, Ra. Omon, can you hear me?"

"Yes, Comrade Flight Leader."

"So far everything seems to be going okay. There was just one difficult moment, when the telemetry malfunctioned. Not that it actually malfunctioned, you understand, they simply activated another system in parallel and the telemetry failed to operate. They even lost control for a few minutes. That was when you were short of air, remember?"

He was speaking in a strange way, quick and excited. I decided he must be feeling very nervous, though just for a moment I suspected he was drunk.

"You gave everyone a good scare, Omon. Sleeping like that. We almost had to postpone the launch."

"I'm sorry, Comrade Flight Leader."

"Never mind, never mind. It's not your fault. They just drugged you too heavily before the trip to Baikonur. So far everything's going just fine."

"Where am I now?"

"On the working trajectory already. You're flying towards the Moon. You mean you slept through the escape from earth orbit, too?"

"I must have. You mean Otto's already..."

"Yes, Otto's gone already. Surely you can see the nose-cone's already separated? But you had to do two extra orbits. Otto panicked at first. He just wouldn't switch on the rockets. We thought he'd chickened out, but then the lad pulled himself together... Anyway, he sent you his regards."

"And Dima?"

"What about Dima? Dima's okay. The automatic landing system isn't used during the inertial section of the flight. Though he still has the corrections to make... Matiushevich, can you hear us?"

"Yes, sir," said Dima's voice in the receiver.

"Okay, you rest for now," said the Flight Leader. "Stand-by tomorrow at 15:00 hours, then correction of trajectory. Over and out."

I put down the receiver and pressed my eyes against the spy-holes to gaze at the blue semi-circle of the Earth. I'd often read how all the cosmonauts were astounded by the sight of our planet from space. They wrote about some fabulously beautiful misty effect, and how the cities with their shining electric lights on the dark side reminded them of huge bonfires, and how they could even see the rivers on the daylight side – well, none of it's true. The thing the Earth seen from space resembles most is a large school globe, like I remembered seeing through the steamed-up glass of a gas-mask. I was soon sick of the sight; I rested my head as comfortably as I could on my arms and went to sleep again.

When I woke up, the Earth was no longer visible. All I could make out through the spy-holes were the white spots of the distant and unattainable stars, blurred by the lenses. I imagined the existence of a huge, immensely hot sphere hanging entirely unsupported in the icy void, billions of kilometres from the closest stars, those tiny gleaming dots, of which all we know is that they exist, and even that's not certain, because a star can die, while its light will carry on travelling out in all directions, so really we don't know anything about stars, except that their life is terrible and senseless, since all their movements through space are predetermined and subject to the laws of mechanics, which leave no hope at all for any chance encounters. But then, I thought, even though we human beings always seem to be meeting each other, and laughing, and slapping each other on the shoulder, and saying goodbye, there's still a certain special dimension into which our consciousness sometimes takes a frightened peep, a dimension in which we also hang quite motionless in a void where there's no up or down, no yesterday or tomorrow, no hope of drawing closer to each other or even exercising our will and changing our fate; we judge what happens to others from the deceptive twinkling light that reaches us, and we spend all our lives journeying towards what we call the light, although its source may have ceased to exist long ago. And me, I thought, all my life I've been journeying towards the moment when I would soar up over the crowds of what the slogans called the workers and the peasants, the soldiers and the intelligentsia, and now here I am hanging in brilliant blackness on the invisible threads of fate and trajectory – and now I see that becoming a heavenly body is not much different from serving a life sentence in a prison carriage that travels round and round a circular railway line without ever stopping.

13

We travelled through space at a speed of two and a half kilometres a second, and the inertial sector of the flight lasted about three days, but I had the feeling I'd been flying for at least a week. Probably because the sun passed in front of the spy-holes several times a day, and every time I was able to watch a quite incredibly beautiful sunrise and sunset.

All that was left now of the immense rocket was the lunar module, made up of the correction and braking stage, where Dima Matiushevich was sitting, and the descent vehicle, that is, the moonwalker on its platform. In order to save fuel, the nose cone had separated before escape from earth orbit, and now there was open space beyond the fuselage of the moonwalker. The lunar module was flying backwards, so to speak, with its main rocket pointing towards the Moon, and gradually the way I felt about it changed just as it had with the cool lift in the Lubyanka building, when it was transformed from a mechanism for going down underground into a device for going up to the surface.

At first the lunar module rose higher and higher above the Earth, until at some point it gradually became clear that it was falling towards the Moon. But there was a difference. In the lift I went down and came up with my head pointing upwards, but I hurtled out of earth orbit with my head pointing downwards; it was only later, after a day or so of the flight, that I found myself with my head upward, falling with ever increasing speed down a black well, clutching the handlebars of my bicycle and waiting for its non-existent wheels to collide silently with the Moon.

I had time for all these thoughts because for the time being I had nothing to do. I often felt like talking to Dima but he was always busy with all his complicated corrections to the trajectory. Sometimes I picked up the receiver and heard his incomprehensible exchanges with the engineers at Central Flight Control:

"Forty-three degrees... Fifty-seven... Yaw..."

I listened to all this for a little while, then gave up on it. As far as I could understand, Dima's main task was to catch the sun in one optical device, the Moon in another, measure something and transmit the result to earth, where they had to check the actual trajectory with the projected one and calculate the length of the corrective impulse required from the engines.

Judging from the fact that I was jerked about quite roughly on my saddle several times, Dima seemed to be coping with his task.

When the shocks stopped, I waited about half an hour, picked up the receiver and called him:

"Hello! Dima!"

"Yes, I hear you," he said in his usual dry manner.

"Have you corrected the trajectory, then?"

"Seems like it."

"Was it difficult?"

"It was fine," he answered.

"Listen," I said, "where did you pick up all that stuff? All those degrees and things? We didn't have any of that in class."

"I served two years in a strategic rocket detachment," he said. "The directional system's much the same, only you use the stars. And without any radio communications – you work it all out yourself on a calculator. Make a mistake and you're fucked."

"And if you don't make a mistake?"

Dima didn't answer that one.

"What were your duties?"

"Operational Officer. Then Strategic Officer."

"What does that mean?"

"Nothing complicated. If you're sitting in a tactical operations rocket, you're an Operational Officer. If you're in a strategic rocket, then you're a Strategic Officer."

"Is it tough?"

"It's okay. Like working as a watchman back in the everyday world. Twenty-four hours' duty in the rocket and three days off."

"So that's what turned your hair grey... I suppose all of you are grey."

Dima didn't answer that one either.

"It's the responsibility, is it?"

"No. More likely the training flights."

"What training flights? Ah – that's when they write in fine print on the back page of *Izvestiya* that it's forbidden to sail into such and such a sector of the Pacific Ocean, is that it?"

"That's it."

"And do they have training flights often?"

"It depends, but you pull a straw every month. Twelve times a year, the entire squadron. All twenty four of you. That's what turns the guys' hair grey."

"And what if you don't want to pull a straw?"

"Pulling a straw is just an expression of speech. What actually happens before the training flight is the Assistant Political Instructor goes round and gives everyone an envelope. Your straw's already in it."

"And if you get a short straw, can you refuse?"

"In the first place, it's a long straw, not a short one. And in the second place, no. All you can do is write an application for a cosmonauts' detachment. But you have to be really lucky."

"Are many people lucky?"

"I've never counted them. I was lucky."

Dima answered my questions reluctantly, with lots of rather impolite pauses. I couldn't think of anything else to ask, so I put down the receiver.

I made my next attempt to talk to him when there were only a few minutes left to braking. I'm ashamed to admit it, but I was overcome by a callous curiosity – would Dima change before..? I wanted to check whether he would be as taciturn as he was during our last conversation, or whether the approaching end of his flight would make him a bit more talkative. I picked up the receiver and called him:

"Dima! This is Omon. Pick up the phone."

The answer I got was:

"Listen, ring me back in two minutes! If your radio's working, switch it on now!"

Dima hung up. His voice sounded excited, and I thought they must be talking about us on the radio. But Radio Beacon was broadcasting music – when I switched on I just caught the fading tinkle of a synthesiser; the programme was just ending, and after a few seconds there was a silent pause. Then came the time signal, and I learned that in a place called Moscow it was two in the afternoon. I waited a bit and then picked up the receiver.

"Did you hear it?" Dima asked excitedly.

"Yes," I said, "but only the very end."

"But did you recognise it?"

"No," I said.

"It was Pink Floyd. 'One of These Days'."

"How come the workers requested that?" I asked in astonishment.

"They didn't, of course," said Dima. "It's the theme tune for the programme 'Life of Science'. From the album 'Meddle'. Pure underground."

"You mean you like Pink Floyd?"

"Me? I'm a fan. I had all their albums. What d'you think of them?"

It was the first time I had heard Dima speak with such enthusiasm.

"Not bad in general," I said. "But not all their stuff. They have this album with a cow on the cover."

"'Atom Heart Mother'," said Dima.

"I like that one. And there's another one I remember – a double album with them sitting in a yard, and on the wall is a picture of the same yard with them sitting in it..."

"'Ummagumma'."

"Maybe. I don't think that's music at all."

"That's right! It's not music, it's shit!" a bass voice roared in the receiver, and we said nothing for a few seconds.

"You're wrong," said Dima when he finally spoke. "At the end there's a new version of 'Saucerful of Secrets'. A different timbre from on 'Nice Pair'. Different singer, too."

I'd forgotten that.

"What do you like on 'Atom Heart Mother'?" asked Dima.

"There are a couple of songs on side two. One's quiet, just a guitar, and the other has an orchestra. The ending's beautiful – tam ta-ta ta-ta ta-ta ta-ta tam-taram tra-ta-ta..."

"I know it," said Dima. "'Summer Sixty-Eight'. And the quiet song's 'If'."

"Maybe," I said. "So what's your favourite record?"

"I don't have a favourite record," Dima said haughtily. "It's not records I like, it's music. On 'Meddle', for instance, I like the first song. About the echo. It makes me cry every time I listen to it. I translated it with a dictionary. 'Overhead the Albatross pa-ra-ram, pa-ram... And help me understand the best I can..."'"

Dima swallowed and fell silent.

"Your English is very good," I said.

"Yes, that's what they told me in the rocket division. The Assistant Political Instructor said so. But that's not the point. There was one record I didn't manage to find. During my last leave I went to Moscow specially, took four hundred roubles with me. I asked around everywhere, no one had even heard of it."

"What record was that?"

"You wouldn't know it. Music from a film. It's called 'Zabriskie Point'."

"Ah," I said, "I did have that one. Not the record, I had it on tape. Nothing special really... Dima, why have you gone all quiet? Hey, Dima!"

The receiver crackled for a long time before Dima asked:

"What's it like?"

"How can I put it?" I said. "Have you heard 'More'?"

"Sure."

"It's kind of like that. Only they don't sing. An ordinary kind of soundtrack. If you've heard 'More', you can reckon you've heard it. Typical Pinky – saxophone, synthesiser. The second side..."

There was a beep in the phone, and my skull cavity was filled with Khalmuradov's loud roar:

"Ra, come in! What are you fucking chattering about up there? Haven't you got anything to do? Prepare the automatic system for soft landing!"

"The automatic system's ready!" Dima replied, reluctantly.

"Then commence orientation of the braking motor axis to the lunar vertical!"

"Alright."

I glanced out into space through the moonwalker's spy-holes and saw the Moon right up close. The picture that met my eyes would have been just like the Ukrainian flag, if its top half was blue instead of black. The phone rang. I picked it up, but it was Khalmuradov again.

"Attention! At the count of three activate the braking motor on the command of the radioaltimeter!"

"Read you," replied Dima.

"One... Two... "

I hung up quickly.

The motor fired. It worked intermittently, and about twenty minutes later my shoulder was suddenly thrown against the wall, then my back was bounced against the ceiling, and then an intolerably loud crash shook everything; I realised that Dima had passed on to immortality without saying goodbye. But I wasn't offended – apart from our final conversation he'd always been taciturn and unsociable, and I had a feeling that sitting for days at a time in the gondola of his intercontinental ballistic missile, he'd understood something which meant he never needed to say hello or goodbye again.

I didn't notice the landing. The shuddering and rumbling suddenly stopped, and looking out through the spy-holes, I saw the same pitch blackness I had seen before the start of the flight. At first I thought something had gone wrong, then I remembered that according to plan I was supposed to land during the lunar night.

I waited for a while, not knowing what I was waiting for. Suddenly the phone rang.

"Khalmuradov here," said the voice. "Is everything in order?"

"Yes sir, Comrade Colonel."

"The telemetry will be activated in a moment, and the guide-rails will be lowered," he said. "You will proceed down on to the surface and report. But use the brakes, you understand?"

Then in a quieter voice, holding the receiver away from his face, he added:

"Hun-der-ground. What a bastard."

The moonwalker swayed and I heard a dull thud from outside.

"Proceed," said Khalmuradov.

This was probably the most difficult part of my assignment – I had to drive down out of the descent module along two narrow guide-rails lowered on to the lunar surface. The guide-rails had special slots to accommodate the flanges on the moonwalker's wheels, so it was impossible to slide off them, but there was still the danger that one of the guide-rails might land on a boulder, and then the moonwalker might tilt and overturn on its way down to the ground. I turned the pedals a few times and felt the massive machine lean forward and begin to move under its own momentum. I pressed the brake, but the force of inertia was too strong, and the moonwalker was dragged downwards; suddenly there was a clanging sound, the brake went slack, and my feet turned the pedals backwards several times with terrifying speed. The moonwalker rolled forward irresistibly, swayed and came to a halt, standing evenly on all eight wheels.

I was on the Moon. But I had no feelings about the fact at all; I was wondering how to put back the chain that had slipped off the cog-wheel. Just when I finally managed it, the phone rang. It was the Flight Leader. His voice sounded solemn and official.

"Comrade Krivomazov! On behalf of the entire aviation officers' corps present here at Central Flight Control, I congratulate you on the soft landing of the Soviet automated space station 'Luna-17B' on the Moon!"

I heard popping sounds, and I realised they were opening champagne. There was music, too – some kind of march; I could hardly hear it, it was almost drowned out by the crackling in the receiver.

14

My youthful dreams of the future were born from the gentle sadness of those evenings, far removed from the rest of life, when you lie in the grass beside the remains of someone else's camp-fire, with your bicycle beside you, watching the purple stripes left in the Western sky by the sun that has just set, and you can see the first stars in the East.

I hadn't seen or experienced very much, but I liked lots of things, and I thought that a flight to the Moon would take in and make up for all the things I had passed by, in hopes of catching up with them later; how could I know that you only ever see the best things in life out of the corner of your eye? As a kid I often imagined the landscapes of other worlds – rocky plains flooded with dead light and pitted with craters; distant, sharp-pointed mountains, a black sky with the huge brand of a sun blazing on it among the glittering stars; I imagined metre-thick layers of cosmic dust, I imagined boulders lying motionless on the surface of the Moon for billions of years – for some reason I was really excited by the idea that a boulder could lie in the same place without moving for so long until one day I bent down and picked it up between the thick fingers of my space suit glove. I thought about how I would raise my head to see the blue sphere of the Earth, and this supreme moment of my life would link me with all the moments when I felt I was standing on the threshold of something wonderful beyond comprehension.

In fact the Moon proved to be a narrow, black, stuffy space where the faint electric light only came on rarely; it turned out to be constant darkness seen through the useless lenses of the spy-holes, and restless, uncomfortable sleep in a cramped position with my head resting on my arms, which lay on the handlebars.

I travelled slowly, about five kilometres a day, and I hadn't the slightest idea what the world around me looked like. But then, of course, this kingdom of eternal darkness probably didn't look like anything – apart from me, there wasn't anybody for whom it could look like anything, and I didn't switch on the headlight, in order to save the battery. The surface of the ground beneath me was obviously even and the machine moved smoothly over it. I couldn't turn the handlebars at all – they must have jammed on landing – so all I had to do was keep turning the pedals. But my journey into space had been so long, that I refused to allow gloomy thoughts to get me down, and I even managed to feel happy.

Hours and days went by. When I halted, it was only to lower my head on to the handlebars and sleep. It was so horribly uncomfortable to use the toilet that I preferred to wait till the final moment, like I used to during quiet hour in kindergarten. The corn beef was gradually running out, there was less and less water in the milk-can; every evening I extended the red line on the map in front of me by another centimetre, and it crept closer and closer to the small black circle where it was supposed to come to a stop. The circle was like the symbol for a metro station; it irritated me that it had no name, and I wrote one beside it – 'Zabriskie Point'.

With my right hand squeezing the nickel-plated knob in the pocket of my padded jacket, I had been staring for an hour at the label of one of the cans, with its words 'Great Wall'. I was having visions of warm winds over the fields of distant China, and I wasn't really interested in the tedious ringing of the phone on the floor, but I picked it up after a while.

"Ra, come in! Why don't you answer? Why aren't we moving? I can see everything here with the telemetry."

"I'm having a rest, Comrade Flight Leader."

"Report the reading on the gauge!"

I glanced at the figures in the opening in the small steel cylinder.

"Thirty-two kilometres, seven hundred metres."

"Now put out the light and listen. Looking at the map here, we can see you're very close."

I felt my heart sink, although I knew there was still a long way to go to that small black circle that gazed at me from the map like the barrel of a gun.

"To what?"

"The landing module of 'Luna-17B'."

"But I'm 'Luna-17B'," I said.

"Never mind, so were they."

It seemed he was drunk again. But I understood what he was talking about. It was the expedition to obtain samples of the lunar soil; that time two cosmonauts had landed on the Moon, Pasiuk Drach and Zurab Pratsvania. They had a small rocket with them which they used to send five hundred grammes of soil back to earth; after that they lived on the lunar surface for one and a half minutes, and then shot themselves.

"Careful, Omon!" said the Flight Leader. "Be cautious now. Reduce speed and switch on the headlights."

I flicked a switch and pressed my eyes to the black lenses of the spy-holes. The optical distortion drew the blackness around the moonwalker into an arch that stretched out ahead of me in

an endless tunnel. All I could make out clearly was a small
section of the rough, uneven rocky surface – it was evidently
ancient basalt; every one and a half metres or so there were
long low outcrops perpendicular to my line of movement; they
reminded me of sand-hills in the desert. The strange thing was I
didn't feel them at all as I moved along.

"Well?" asked the voice in the receiver.

"I don't see anything," I said.

"Turn off the headlights and proceed. Don't hurry."

I went on for another forty minutes. Then the moonwalker
collided with something. I picked up the phone.

"Earth, come in. There's something here."

"Switch on the headlights."

Right in the centre of my field of vision lay two hands in
black leather gloves. The extended fingers of the right hand lay
over the handle of a small shovel which still held a little sand
mixed with small stones, and the left hand gripped a 'Makarov'
pistol that gleamed dully. There was something dark between
the hands. Looking closer, I could make out the raised collar of
an officer's padded jacket with the top of a fur cap protruding
above it; the man's shoulder and part of his head were
concealed by the wheel of the moonwalker.

"What is it, Omon?" the receiver breathed in my ear.

I described briefly what I could see.

"What about the epaulettes, can you see them?"

"No, I can't."

"Move back half a metre."

"The moonwalker doesn't travel backwards," I said. "It has
pedal braking."

"Damn... I told the chief designer," mumbled the Flight
Leader. "I wonder who it is, Zura or Pasha. Zura was a
captain, and Pasha was a major. Okay, switch off the
headlights, you'll flatten the batteries."

"Yes sir," I said, but before I carried out the order, I took
another look at the motionless hand and the fabric top of the
fur cap. I couldn't get moving for a while, but then I gritted my
teeth and put all my weight on the pedal. The moonwalker
jerked upwards and then, a second later, back down again.

"Proceed," said Khalmuradov, who had replaced the Flight

Leader on the phone. "You're falling behind schedule."

I saved energy by spending almost all the time in total darkness, frenziedly turning the pedals and only switching on the light for a few seconds at a time in order to check the compass, although this was quite pointless, since the handlebars were useless anyway. But they ordered me to do it. It's hard to describe the sensation: darkness, a hot, cramped space, sweat dripping from your brow, a gentle swaying – perhaps an embryo experiences something of the sort in its mother's womb.

I was aware that I was on the Moon, but the immense distance separating me from the Earth was a pure abstraction for me. I felt as though the people I spoke with on the phone were somewhere close by – not because I could hear their voices clearly in the receiver, but because I couldn't imagine how the entirely immaterial official relationships and personal feelings that linked us together could be stretched so far. But the strangest thing was that the memories connecting me with childhood could extend over such an incomprehensible distance too.

When I went to school, I used to spend the summers in a village outside Moscow. It stood on the edge of a main highway, and I spent most of my time in the saddle of my bike, sometimes riding up to thirty or forty kilometres a day. The bicycle wasn't very well adjusted – the handlebars were too low, and I really had to bend down to them – like in the moonwalker. And now, probably because my body had been set in that pose for such a long time, I began having light hallucinations. I seemed to drift off into a waking sleep – in the darkness it was particularly easy – and I dreamed I could see my shadow on the asphalt rushing past below me, and the white dotted line in the middle of the highway, and I was breathing air smelling of diesel fumes. I began to think I could hear the roar of lorries rushing past and the hissing of tyres on asphalt, and only the next radio contact brought me back to my senses. But afterwards I dropped out of lunar reality and again was transported back to the Moscow highway, and I realised how much the hours I spent there had meant to me.

On one occasion Comrade Kondratiev came on the radio to talk to me and began declaiming poetry about the Moon. I was wondering how to ask him to stop without being offensive, when he began reading a poem that I recognised from the very first lines as a photographic image of my soul:

"Life's vital bonds we took for lasting truth,
But as I turn my head to glance at you,
How strangely changed you are, my early youth,
Your colours are not mine, and not one line is true.
And in my mind, moonglow is what I see
Between us two, the drowning man and shallow place;
Your semi-racer bears you off from me
Along the miles towards the Moon's bright face,
How long now since..."

I gave a quiet sob, and Comrade Kondratiev immediately stopped.

"What comes next?" I asked.

"I've forgotten," said Comrade Kondratiev. "It's gone clean out of my head."

I didn't believe him, but I knew it was pointless to argue or plead.

"What are you thinking about now?" he asked.

"Nothing really," I said.

"Nobody thinks of nothing," he said. "There's always some thought or other running round your head. Tell me, I'd like to know."

"Well, I often remember my childhood," I said reluctantly. "How I used to go riding on my bike. It was a lot like this. And to this day I don't understand it – there I was, riding along on my bike, with the handlebars way down low, and it was really bright up ahead, and the wind was so fresh..."

I stopped speaking.

"Well? What is it you don't understand?"

"I thought I was riding towards the canal... So how can it be that I?.."

Comrade Kondratiev said nothing for a minute or two and

then quietly put down the receiver.

I switched on Radio Beacon – I didn't believe it was really Beacon, even though every two minutes they assured me it was.

"Maria Ivanovna Plakhuta from the village of Nukino has given the Motherland seven sons," said a woman's voice, soaring out over the factory lunchtime in distant Russia. "Two of them, Ivan Plakhuta and Vassily Plakhuta, are now serving in the army, in the tank forces of the KGB. They have asked us to broadcast the comic song 'The Samovar' for their mother. We're doing just as you asked, lads. Maria Ivanovna, here singing for you is People's Jester of the USSR, Artem Plakhuta, who was just as delighted to accept our invitation as he was to be demobilised from the army with the rank of senior sergeant eight years before his brothers."

Then the balalaikas began to jangle, the cymbals clashed a couple of times, and a voice filled with feeling, leaning hard on the letter "r" as if it was the person crushed next to him in a crowded bus, began to sing:

"O-oh, the wa-terrr's on the boil!"

I switched it off. The words sent a shiver through me. I remembered Dima's grey head, and the cow on the cover of 'Atom Heart Mother', and a cold shudder ran slowly down my spine. I waited a minute or two until I was sure the song must have finished, and turned the black knob. For a second there was silence, and then the baritone leapt out of hiding straight into my face with:

"We gave the skunks our tea to drink,
Fed them water fiery hot!"

This time I waited longer, and when I finally switched the radio on, the announcer was speaking:

"Let us remember our cosmonauts, and all those whose earthly labours make possible their shift-work in the heavens. For them today..."

I withdrew into my own thoughts, or rather, I suddenly found myself immersed in one of them, as though I had fallen through thin ice, and I only began to hear anything again a few minutes later, as a ponderous choir of distant basses was laying the final bricks in the monumental edifice of a new song. But even though I was completely unaware of the real world, I carried on mechanically pressing the pedals, with my right knee turned out as far as possible – that way I felt less pain from the blister my boot had given me.

I was struck by a sudden idea.

If now, when I closed my eyes, I was – as far as a person can actually be anywhere – on a phantom highway outside Moscow, and the nonexistent asphalt, trees and sunshine became as real to me as though I actually was dashing down a slope in my favourite second gear; if – forgetting about Zabriskie Point, which was not very far off now – I was sometimes happy for a few seconds, didn't that mean that already back then in my childhood, when I was simply a part of a world submerged in summer happiness, when I really was dashing along the asphalt strip on my bicycle, riding against the wind into the sun, without the slightest interest in what the future had in store for me – didn't that mean that even then I was really already trundling across the black, lifeless surface of the Moon, seeing nothing but what penetrated into conscious-ness through the crooked spy-holes as the moonwalker slowly solidified around me?

> *"We're spaceward bound tomorrow*
> *But there's no grief or sorrow*
> *Alone in the sky.*
> *The Moon's riding high.*
> *You ripe ears of barley, good-bye."*

15

I saw a board on the wall bearing a pointy-bearded golden profile and the word "Lenin", written in a semicircle and framed by two metal-foil olive branches. Although I'd walked past the spot plenty of times before, there had always been people around, and I hadn't dared go right up close.

I scanned the entire structure with a new interest: the board was quite large – about a metre high – and covered with crimson velvet. It hung from two hinges, and a small hook on the back held it right up against the wall. I glanced around. Quiet hour wasn't over yet, and there was no one in the corri-

dor. I went over to the window – the avenue leading to the
dining-hall was empty, except for two moonwalkers at the far
end, slowly creeping towards me. I recognised the camp
leaders, Yura and Lena. It was quiet, the only sound was the
tapping of a table-tennis ball downstairs: I was filled with
melancholy at the idea that someone had the right to play
table-tennis during the quiet hour. Then I unlatched the hook
and pulled the board towards myself, revealing a square section
of the wall. Right in the centre of it I saw a switch, painted
with gold paint. The hollow churning in the pit of my stomach
grew even worse as I reached out and flicked the switch
upwards.

There was a low buzzing sound. Without even knowing
what it was, I felt like I'd done something terrible to the world
around me, and to myself as well. The buzzer sounded again,
louder this time, and suddenly I realised that the switch, the
small crimson door I'd opened, and the corridor I was standing
in – none of it was real, because I wasn't really standing by a
switch on a wall, but sitting uncomfortably hunched over in
some terribly cramped space. There was another buzz, and a
few seconds later the moonwalker materialised around me.
One more buzz, and the thought flitted through my mind that
yesterday, before I lowered my head on to the handlebars, I
had extended the red line on the map to the centre of the black
circle beside the words 'Zabriskie Point'.

The phone was ringing.

"Sleep well, you ass-hole?" Colonel Khalmuradov's voice
thundered in the receiver.

"Ass-hole yourself," I said, suddenly angry.

Khalmuradov gave a rumbling, infectious laugh – I realised
he wasn't offended at all.

"I'm all alone again here in Central Flight Control. The
lads have gone off to Japan to set up a joint flight mission.
Pkhadzer Vladlenovich sends you his regards, says he was sorry
he didn't get to say goodbye – it was all decided at the last
moment. And I had to stay here all because of you. Well, are
you setting up the radio-buoy today? Probably had enough,
have you? Glad it's over?"

I didn't answer.

"What's this, are you angry with me? Omon? Just because I called you a wanker that time? Forget it, will you? You had all Central Flight Control shitting bricks, we almost had to cancel the flight," said Khalmuradov. He paused, then went on. "You act just like a stupid woman... Are you a man or not? Today's a special day. Just you remember that."

"I remember," I said.

"Button yourself up as tight as you can," Khalmuradov advised me anxiously, "especially the neck of your jacket. Your face..."

"I know what to do as well as you," I interrupted.

"First you put on the goggles, then you wrap the scarf round your head, and then you put on your cap. Be sure to fasten it under your chin. Then the gloves. Tie your sleeves and your boots with string – you can't mess around with a vacuum. Then you'll be able to last three minutes. Understood?"

"Understood."

"Not 'understood', you bastard – 'yes, sir'. Report back when you're ready."

They say that during the last minutes of his life a man sees it all again in fast rewind. I don't know about that. Nothing of the sort happened to me, no matter how hard I tried. What I saw instead was a vivid, strangely detailed picture of Landratov in Japan – walking along the street in the morning sunshine wearing brand-new expensive training shoes, and smiling – probably not even remembering what kind of feet he was wearing them on. And I imagined the others – the Flight Leader, transformed into an elderly intellectual in a three-piece suit, and Comrade Kondratiev, giving a thoughtful interview to a correspondent from the television current affairs programme. But not a single thought about myself entered my head. To calm myself down, I switched on the radio and listened to a quiet song about lights burning in the distance beyond the river, a head lowered in sorrow, a heart pierced by grief, and White Guards who had nothing to lose but their golden watch-chains.

Suddenly the radio was switched off and the phone rang.

"Well," asked Khalmuradov, "are you ready?"

"Not yet," I answered, "what's the hurry?"

"You little jerk, you," said Khalmuradov, "I saw what it said in your personal file about you not having any childhood friends except for that bastard we shot. Don't you ever think about other people? I could miss my tennis again."

Somehow I found it incredibly offensive to think that in a short while Khalmuradov would be standing on the courts at Luzhniki with white shorts on his fat thighs, knocking a tennis ball around the asphalt, while I wouldn't be around any more. I didn't feel this because I envied him, but because I suddenly recalled with startling clarity a certain sunny September day in that same Luzhniki, when I was still at school. But then I realised that when I was gone, Khalmuradov and Luzhniki itself would be gone too, and the thought dispelled the melancholy my dream had left with me.

"Other people? What other people?" I asked quietly.

"Anyway, it's no big deal. You go. I'll manage on my own."

"Stop that."

"It's alright, you go."

"Stop it, stop it," Khalmuradov said in a serious voice. "I have to finalise the report, register the signal from the Moon, note the time in Moscow. Just you get on with it."

"Is Landratov in Japan too?" I suddenly asked.

"What's that you asked?" Khalmuradov said suspiciously.

"I just remembered something."

"So, what was it you remembered? Tell me."

"I just remembered him dancing the 'Kalinka' at the graduation exams."

"I get you. Hey, Landratov, are you in Japan? Someone here's asking for you."

There was a sound of laughter and the slippery squeak of fingers on the receiver.

"He's here," Khalmuradov said at last. "He sends his regards."

"Give him mine too. Alright, I suppose it's time."

"Push open the hatch," Khalmuradov said quickly, repeating the instructions I knew off by heart, "and immediately grab the handlebars so the air pressure won't throw you out. Then take a breath from the oxygen mask through the scarf and climb out. Walk fifteen steps along the line of motion, take out the radio-buoy, set it down and turn it on. Make sure you carry it a good distance, or the moonwalker will screen the signal... And then... We've given you a pistol with a single bullet, and we've never had any cowards in the cosmonauts' detachment yet."

I hung up. The telephone rang again, but I took no notice. For a second I toyed with the idea of not switching on the radio-buoy so that bastard Khalmuradov would have to hang around in Central Flight Control till the end of the day, and then collect some kind of Party reprimand, but I remembered Sema Anikin and how he said I had to get there and finish the job. I couldn't betray the guys from the first and second stages, not even unsociable Dima; they'd died so I could be here now, and in the face of their exalted destiny my spiteful feelings for Khalmuradov seemed petty and shameful. And when I finally knew that in a few seconds I would gather my courage and do what had to be done, the phone stopped ringing.

I began making preparations and in half an hour I was ready. I sealed my ears and nostrils tightly with the special hydrocompensatory tampons made of greased cotton-wool and then checked my outfit – everything was buttoned up tight, tucked in and tied down; the rubber strap of the motorcycle goggles was a little too tight, and they bit into my face, but I didn't try fiddling with them: I wouldn't have to put up with it for very long anyway. I picked up the holster from the shelf, drew out the pistol, cocked it and shoved it into the pocket of my padded jacket. I threw the sack with the radio-buoy over my left shoulder, and was just about to pick up the phone when I remembered I'd already sealed my ears with cotton wool; and anyway, I didn't really want to waste my final moments of life on conversation with Khalmuradov. I remembered the last time I talked to Dima and I was sure I had done the right thing by lying to him about 'Zabriskie Point'. It's a miserable thing to leave behind a world which still holds secrets.

I breathed out, as though I was about to jump into deep water, and set to work.

After all those hours of training, my body knew what it had to do so well that I didn't stop once, even though I had to work in almost total darkness, because the battery was so flat the lamp had stopped giving out light – I could just make out the little crimson worm of the filament. First I had to remove five bolts around the edge of the hatch. When the final bolt clanged against the floor, I felt along the wall for the little window over the emergency opening switch and hit the glass hard with my last tin of corn beef. The glass shattered. I stuck my hand in through the opening, hooked my finger into the ring of the explosive cartridge and tugged. The cartridge was made with explosives from an 'F-1' grenade, and it had a three second delay, so there was just enough time for me to grab the handlebars and get my head down as low as possible. There was a thunderous bang above my head and I was shaken so hard I was almost thrown out of the saddle, but I managed to hold on. I waited half a second and raised my head.

There above me was the black bottomless abyss of open space. The only thing between me and it was the thin plexiglass of my motorcycle goggles. I was surrounded by total darkness. I bent down, took a deep breath from the oxygen mask, scrambled clumsily out of the moonwalker, stood up and began walking – every step cost an immense effort to overcome the pain in my back, which I hadn't straightened up for a month. I didn't feel like walking the full fifteen steps, so I went down on one knee, loosened the string around the sack with the radio-buoy and started pulling it out, but the lever got jammed and I couldn't shift it. It was getting harder and harder to hold the air in my lungs, and I had a brief moment of panic – I thought I would die there and then, without finishing the job I had come to do. But the next moment the sack slipped off, I set the radio-buoy on the invisible surface of the Moon and turned the lever. Out into the ether flew the encoded words "Lenin", "USSR" and "Peace", repeated every three seconds, and a tiny red lamp sprang to life on the side of the buoy, lighting up an image of the Earth floating across ears of barley – and for the first time in my life I noticed that my Motherland's national emblem showed the view from the Moon.

The air was bursting out of my lungs, and I knew in a few seconds I would let go and my scorched mouth would choke on emptiness. I swung back my arm and threw the nickel-plated bed-knob as far as I could. It was time to die. I took the pistol out of my pocket, raised it to my temple and tried to remember the most important event of my brief existence, but the only thing that came into my head was the story of Marat Popadya as his father told it to me. I was offended by the absurdity of dying with a thought that had nothing to do with me, and I tried to think of something else, but I couldn't; I could see the clearing in the winter forest, the huntsmen sitting in the bushes, the two bears roaring as they rushed at the hunters – and as I pressed the trigger, I suddenly realised beyond a shadow of a doubt that Kissinger had very well known what he was stabbing at.

The pistol misfired, but it wasn't needed anyway; there were bright-coloured life-belts drifting in front of my eyes, I tried to grab one of them, missed and collapsed onto the black, ice-cold lunar basalt.

I felt a sharp stone sticking into my cheek – it wasn't all that painful through the scarf, but it was unpleasant enough. I propped myself up on my elbows and looked around. I could not see a thing. My nose began to itch; I sneezed, and one of the tampons flew out of my nostril. Then I pulled off the scarf, the goggles and the cap and dragged the swollen cotton-wool tampons out of my ears and nose. I couldn't hear anything, but there was a distinct musty smell. It was damp and cold – despite the padded jacket.

I stood up and fumbled round about me, then stretched out my arms and started walking forward. Almost immediately I stumbled over something, but I kept my balance. A few steps later my fingers came up against a wall; I moved my hands along it and felt a thick festoon of wires covered in sticky fluff. I turned and walked in the opposite direction, walking more carefully this time, lifting my feet high in the air, but after a few steps I stumbled over something again. Again my hands felt a wall with cables hanging on it. Then I noticed a tiny red lamp lighting up a five-sided metal object about five metres away from me – and I remembered everything.

But before I could come to terms with what I remembered or think clearly about anything, there was a flash of light far off to my right; I turned my head, instinctively shielding my face with my hands, and through the gaps between my fingers I saw a tunnel running off into the distance – the bright light was at the far end of it, and it lit up the thick bunches of cables covering the walls and the rails that ran together in a distant point.

Turning away from the light, I saw the moonwalker standing on the rails, painted all over in stars and emblazoned with the letters "USSR", and my own long black shadow falling across it. I stumbled towards it, shielding my face from the blinding light drifting towards me above the rails – somehow it suddenly reminded me of the setting sun. Something ricocheted off the fuselage of the moonwalker, at the very same instant as I heard a loud crack; I realised I was being shot at and made a dash for shelter behind the moonwalker. Another bullet clanged against the fuselage, and it went on ringing for several seconds, like a funeral bell. I heard the clatter of wheels, then there was another shot, and the clattering of wheels stopped.

"Hey, Krivomazov!" thundered an inhumanly loud voice. "Come out with your hands up, you bastard! They've given you a medal!"

I peeped out from behind the moonwalker: standing on the rails about fifty metres away was a small hand-trolley with a blinding search-light, and swaying to and fro in front of it on wide-straddled legs was a man with a megaphone in one hand and a pistol in the other. He raised the gun: a shot rang out like thunder and the bullet ricocheted several times before it whistled past just below the roof. I hid my head.

"Come on out, you skunk!"

His voice was familiar, but I couldn't quite tell who it was. "Two!"

He fired again, and hit the fuselage of the moonwalker. "Three!"

I peeped out again and saw him put the megaphone on his trolley, stretch out his arms to the sides and begin to jog slowly over the sleepers towards the moonwalker. When he got a bit closer, I could hear him making buzzing noises with his mouth, imitating the roar of aeroplane engines, and I recognised him straight away – it was Landratov. I would have backed away down the tunnel, but I realised that as soon as he reached the moonwalker, I would be absolutely defenceless. I hesitated for a second, then bent down and dived under the low hull.

All I could see now were his legs coming closer and closer, stepping deftly but somehow sloppily over the sleepers. He didn't seem to have noticed anything. When he got close to the moonwalker, he began buzzing differently, with a more intense sound, and I realised he was banking steeply as he rounded the machine. His boot appeared between the rusty wheels and without having planned it, I grabbed his legs. When my fingers closed around his ankles, the sensation of almost total emptiness in his boots was so nauseating I nearly let go of them again. He shouted and fell. I didn't loosen my grip, and the artificial limbs twisted unnaturally in the soft leather. I gave them one more twist and crawled out from under the moonwalker; by the time I was free of it, he was already crawling towards his pistol, which had fallen between the sleepers. I had only a second left; I grabbed the heavy five-sided radio-buoy and smashed it down on the back of Landratov's yellow-haired head.

There was a crunching sound, and the little red lamp went out.

Landratov's hand-trolley was a lot lighter than my moonwalker and it moved a lot faster. The powerful searchlight lit up the round gallery and the cables running along its walls, all with a sticky covering of some kind of tacky fibres. As far as I could tell, the gallery was an abandoned metro tunnel. At several points other tunnels branched off from it, just as dark and lifeless as the one I was travelling along. Occasionally rats ran across ahead – some of them were as big as small dogs – but they paid no attention to me, thank God. Then came a side-tunnel on the right, just like the others, but as I got close, the trolley jerked so sharply to the right that I flew off on to the rails and bruised my shoulder badly.

The points I'd just ridden over were set in a halfway position, so that the front wheels went straight ahead while the back wheels went to the right; as a result, the trolley was jammed solid. I knew I had to go on in the darkness on foot, and I began slowly feeling my way forward, regretting that I hadn't picked up Landratov's pistol, though it would hardly have saved me from the rats if they decided to attack.

Before I'd gone fifty metres I heard shouting and dogs barking ahead of me. I turned and ran back the way I'd come. Lights came on behind me; turning to look, I saw the grey forms of two alsatians leaping over the sleepers ahead of the swaying circles of torchlight which were all I could see of my pursuers.

"There he is! Belka! Strelka! Get him!" someone yelled behind me.

I turned into the side tunnel and set off as fast as I could, striding high so I wouldn't break my legs. I stepped on a rat and almost fell, then suddenly I saw the bright unwinking points of unearthly stars shining off to my right. I dashed towards them, collided with a wall and clambered over it, clutching at the cables, and all the while feeling the alsatians rushing at my back. I tumbled over the top of the wall and fell, and the only reason I didn't hurt myself was that I landed on something very soft, which felt like an armchair covered in polythene. I squeezed into a crevice between some boxes and crates and began creeping along it; several times my hands knocked against the backs of chairs and the arms of armchairs wrapped in polythene. Suddenly it was brighter. I heard a quiet conversation very close by and I froze. Right in front of my face was the back panel of a wardrobe – a large sheet of hardboard with the word "Nevka" stamped on it. I heard barks and shouting behind me, and then a loud voice amplified by a megaphone:

"Stop that! Quiet! We're on the air in two minutes!"

The dogs carried on barking, and an insolent tenor voice tried to explain what the problem was, but the megaphone started roaring again:

"Fuck off out of here if you and your dogs don't want to be court-martialled!"

The barking gradually faded – obviously the dogs had been dragged away. After a minute I felt brave enough to peep out from behind the wardrobe.

At first I thought I must be in some huge ancient Roman

planetarium. On an immensely high vaulted ceiling, set among glass and tin, the distant stars glimmered at about one-third of full voltage. About forty metres from the wardrobe stood an old crane; attached to its lifting arm, about four metres above the ground, was a Salyut spacecraft, shaped like a huge bottle. Docked with the Salyut was an Agdam T-3 cargo shuttle; the spaceship sat on the lifting arm the way a plastic model aeroplane sits on its stand. The entire structure was obviously too heavy for the crane to support, because the stern of the cargo shuttle was supported by a couple of long beams braced against the floor; I could just make them out in the half-light, but when two floodlights came on right beside the wardrobe, they became almost invisible because, like the wall behind them, they were painted black and covered with pieces of glittering foil that reflected the electric light.

The floodlights were fitted with filters, and their light was a strange, deathly white. Apart from the spaceship, which immediately looked very convincing, they also lit up a television camera and two machine-gunners who were smoking beside it, and a long table with microphones, food and spectrally transparent bottles of vodka looking like icicles that had been hammered through the table; sitting at the table were two generals. At one side stood a table with a microphone, at which a man in civilian clothes was sitting. Behind him was a large sheet of plywood with the word "News" and a drawing of the Earth; rising crookedly over the Earth was a five-pointed star with long, extended side-rays. Another civilian was leaning over the table and talking to the man behind the microphone.

"Double three!"

I didn't see who said that. The second civilian ran over to the camera and pointed it towards the small table. A bell rang, and the man at the microphone began to speak:

"Today we are at the front line of Soviet space science, in one of the branches of Central Flight Control. Cosmonauts Armen Vezirov and Djambul Mezhelaitis are now in their seventh year on board an orbital spacecraft. This is the longest space flight in history, and it has put our country at the forefront of world space technology. It is symbolic that I should be here with cameraman Nikolai Gordienko on the very day when the cosmonauts are carrying out an important scientific assignment – in exactly thirty seconds they will emerge from their craft into open space in order to install the 'Quantum' astrophysics module."

The entire space was suddenly illuminated by a soft, diffused light – I raised my head and saw that the lamps on the ceiling had been turned up to full voltage, revealing a magnificent panorama of the starry sky to which man has aspired for so many centuries, the inspiration for those beautiful but naive legends about silver nails driven into the firmament.

There was the sound of muffled blows from the direction of the Salyut – the sound of a shoulder hammering on a cellar door which is swollen from damp, when the person opening it is afraid of overturning the pots of sour cream just inside. Finally I saw the door of the hatch projecting slightly above the fuselage of the spaceship, and the man at the table with the microphone spoke:

"Attention, we're going live!"

The hatch slowly opened, and a round silvery helmet with a short antenna appeared above the side of the spaceship. Everyone at the table applauded; the helmet was followed by shoulders and a pair of silvery arms – the first thing they did was attach a safety line to the special bracket on the fuselage; their movements were very slow and smooth, perfected by long hours of training in the swimming pool. Finally the first cosmonaut clambered out into open space and stopped a few steps away from the hatch. I thought it must take quite a lot of courage to stand like that four metres above the ground. Then I had the impression that one of the generals at the table was looking in my direction, and I pulled my head in behind the wardrobe. When I shoved it back out again, both cosmonauts were standing on the spaceship, their suits blindingly white against the inky-black background of the cosmic abyss, scattered with the tiny points of stars. One of them was holding a small box; the cosmonauts moved with a slow, underwater gait along the fuselage of the spaceship to a tall mast, and quickly screwed the box to it. Then they turned to face the television cameras, waved their hands smoothly, walked back to the hatch with that same underwater stride, and one after the other disappeared inside.

The hatch closed, but I went on and on staring at the stars glittering so unimaginably far away – at the long slim arms of the constellation of the Swan, uncertain whether to embrace the huge Pegasus which covered half the sky, or the small, but touchingly pure and clear Lyra.

The man in civilian clothes was speaking rapidly and happily into his microphone:

"While the operation was in progress there was silence here at Central Flight Control. I must confess I was holding my breath too, but everything went to plan. One has to marvel at the cosmonauts' precision and coordination – the years of training and orbital flight have clearly not been wasted. The scientific equipment installed today..."

I crept behind the wardrobe. I felt apathetic, indifferent to everything. If they had tried to catch me then, I probably wouldn't have bothered to run for it or even resist; the only thing I wanted to do was sleep. Following my moonside habit, I rested my head on my folded arms and dozed off. Through my sleep I heard a voice:

"This television broadcast of men at work in open space came from a camera installed by the flight engineer on one of the main unit's solar batteries."

I slept for a long time, maybe five hours. A few times someone began moving things around and swearing close by, then a thin female voice said the divan had to be changed, but I didn't budge – I could have been dreaming. When I finally came round, everything was quiet. I stood up cautiously and glanced out from behind the wardrobe. There was no one at the table with the microphone, and the television camera was covered with a groundsheet. One floodlight lit up the spaceship. I couldn't see anyone there. I came out from behind the wardrobe and looked around: everything was just the same as during the television broadcast, but now I noticed there was quite a large pile of garbage under the spaceship – horrible scraps of white paper and empty tins.

I went over to the table, to the left-over vodka and plates of hors d'oeuvres; I wanted a drink badly. When I sat down, my back automatically hunched over into the bicycle posture; I straightened up with considerable effort, and poured all the left-over vodka together – there was enough for two full glasses, and I drank them down one after the other. For several seconds I thought about following it with one of the marinated mushrooms left on the plate, but the sight of a fork covered in sticky slime made me feel squeamish.

I remembered my crew-mates, and imagined a hall like this one, with zinc coffins standing on the floor – four soldered shut and one still empty. I supposed in some ways the others were happier than me, but I still felt sad for them. Then I thought about Mitiok. Pretty soon I got this buzzing in my head, and I found I could think about what had happened that day. But instead of doing that, I remembered my last day on earth, with the rain darkening the cobblestones on Red Square, Colonel Urchagin's wheelchair, and his warm lips brushing my ear as he whispered:

"I know how hard it was for you to lose your friend and learn that ever since you were a child you had been approaching your moment of immortality arm in arm with a cunning and experienced enemy – I won't even pronounce his name. But remember a certain conversation at which the three of us were present, when he said: 'What does it matter what thought a man dies with? We're materialists, after all.' You remember I said that after he dies a man lives on in the fruit of his deeds. But there is something else I didn't say, something even more important. Remember, Omon, although man, of course, has no soul, every soul is a universe. That's the dialectic. And as long as there is a single soul in which our cause lives and conquers, that cause will never die. For an entire universe will exist, and at its centre will be this..."

He gestured across the square, where the cobblestones gleamed, black and menacing.

"And now for the most important thing you must remember, Omon. You can't understand what I'm going to say yet, but I'm saying it for a moment that will come later, when I won't be beside you. So listen. Just one pure and honest soul is enough for our country to take the lead in the conquest of space; just one pure soul is enough for the banner of triumphant socialism to be unfurled on the surface of the distant Moon. But there must be one pure soul, if only for a moment, because the banner will be unfurled within that soul…"

Suddenly, I caught a powerful smell of sweat and started to turn around, only to be knocked from my chair by a blow from a fist in a thick rubber glove.

A figure towered over me in a tattered felt spacesuit and a helmet with the letters "USSR" painted on its rim in red. He grabbed an empty bottle, smashed it against the table and leant down over me with the jagged edge in his raised hand; I managed to roll away, jump to my feet and run for it. He set off after me – although his movements were very slow, he still managed to move very fast, in a way that was terrifying. I spotted his companion out of the corner of my eye – he was hurriedly clambering down one of the black beams propping up the Agdam T-3, knocking off the tin-foil stars as he went. I ran to the doors and charged them with my shoulder, but they were locked. I ran back and dodged past the first cosmonaut, only to run straight into the second, who swung his leg and kicked at me with a boot with a heavy magnetic sole. He aimed for the groin, but hit me on the leg – and then tried to butt me in the stomach with the sharp antenna on his helmet. I managed to dodge away again. It was then I realised I'd drunk the vodka they had probably been looking forward to for years, and I felt really scared. Ahead of me I saw a small door with the word "Danger" painted on it, and a bolt of lightning inside a triangle. I ran for it.

Behind the door was a very narrow corridor with a rumbling iron floor. I forced myself to run about five metres along it, and then I heard again the heavy clanging of magnetic soles behind my back. That gave me speed and strength: I turned a corner and saw a short corridor ending in the round opening of a ventilation shaft with its wire grille torn away. Beyond the opening stood a motionless rusty fan-blade. As I turned to run back, I was so close to my pursuer I didn't even sense him as a single whole, just a collection of unrelated impressions: a sphere with a bottle-green plexiglass visor and huge red letters, a black rubber glove with a small transparent trident protruding from it, a powerful smell of sweat, and a major's epaulettes on silver-painted felt. The next instant I was already squirming into the ventilation shaft behind the wire netting; I squeezed pretty quickly between the blades of the huge fan, like a ship's propeller, but when I began climbing into the shaft that led upwards and away, my padded jacket bunched up and I got stuck there, squirming like an embryo in the womb. There was a rustling sound below me and something touched my ankle. I shouted and jerked myself free and upwards, covering two metres in a matter of seconds and then squeezing into a horizontal branch of the shaft. It ended in a round opening, and beyond that I could see the Earth swathed in whispy clouds; I sobbed and crawled towards it.

Through the film of my tears the Earth was blurred and indistinct and it seemed to be suspended in a yellowish void; I watched its surface draw closer from out of this void as I squirmed my way towards it, until the walls that were pressing in on me parted, and the brown tiles of the floor flew up to meet me.

"Hey you, mister!" I opened my eyes. A woman in a dirty blue smock was bending over me; a bucket stood on the floor beside her, and she had a mop in her hand.

"Feeling bad, are you? What d'you want here?"

I looked around me – in the wall opposite me there was a small brown door. Beside it hung a calendar with a big photograph of the Earth and the words "For Peace in Space!" I was lying in a short corridor with blue-painted walls, with three or four doors close by. Looking up, I saw the black opening of a ventilation shaft in the wall opposite the calendar.

"Eh?" I asked.

"I said, you drunk, are you?"

Supporting myself against the wall, I got to my feet and set off along the corridor.

"Where d'you think you're going?" the woman said, and turned me round roughly. I set off in the opposite direction. Around the corner there was a steep staircase leading upwards, which ended in a wooden door. Beyond the door there was an indistinct buzz of noise.

"Go on," said the woman, pushing me from behind.

I walked up the steps and then looked round – she was watching me carefully from the bottom of the stairs. I pushed the door and found myself standing in a dark niche behind several people in civilian clothes. They took no notice of me. There was a distant rumbling sound, gradually growing louder. Glancing sideways, I read an inscription in bronze letters – "Lenin Library".

The thought suddenly hit me – Earth!

I stepped out of the cubby-hole under the stairs and staggered slowly along the metro platform towards the large mirror at its far end. Above the mirror menacing orange digits spelled out the time, informing me that it was not yet evening, but time was getting on, and the previous train had passed through just over four minutes ago. The face of a young man with stubble that hadn't seen a razor in ages was staring at me out of the mirror; his eyes were inflamed and his hair was a tangled mess. He was wearing a dirty black padded jacket, smeared in places with whitewash, and he looked as though he'd spent last night far from a bed.

A policeman with a small moustache who was striding up and down the hall began giving me the eye, and when a train arrived and the doors opened, I stepped in through the opening without a second thought. The doors closed, and the train carried me off into a new life. The flight continues, I thought. Half the lamps in the moonwalker weren't working, which sort of soured the light. I sat down; the woman beside me automatically squeezed her legs together, moved away from me, and set her string shopping bag in the space between us. From the corner of my eye, I noticed a box of macaroni stars and the sad, small shape of a frozen chicken.

I had to decide where to go. I looked up at the metro diagram on the wall beside the emergency-stop handle, and began to work out where exactly on the red line I was.

Moscow, 1992

The Yellow Arrow

Andrei was woken by the usual morning noises: cheerful conversation in the toilet queue, which already filled the corridor, the desperate crying of a child behind the thin partition wall, and his neighbour's snoring. For several minutes he attempted to struggle against the onset of day, but then the radio came on and began playing music that sounded like it was being poured into the atmosphere from a huge saucepan by some gigantic cook.

"The most important thing," said the invisible speaker right beside his head, "is the mood in which you enter on the new morning. Popular Estonian singer Guna Tamas wishes you a relaxed and joyful day, filled with sunshine."

Andrei swung his legs down on to the floor and felt for his shoes. Petr Sergeievich was still snoring on the bunk-bed opposite. Judging from the energetic heaving of his shoulders and backside under the sheet marked with blue triangular stamps, he intended to spend at least another hour in the embrace of sleep. Petr Sergeievich was clearly impervious to Guna Tamas's morningtime greetings and the voices in the corridor, but his invisible armour was no help to anyone else, and for Andrei the new day had irrevocably begun.

Dressing quickly and drinking down a few mouthfuls of cold tea, he jerked his towel embroidered with a double-headed cock off its hook, picked up the plastic carrier bag holding his toiletries, and went out into the corridor. The last person in the toilet queue was a bearded Caucasian by the name of Abel – today for some reason his face didn't have its usual affable expression, and even the toothbrush protruding from his fist seemed like a short dagger.

"I'm behind you in line," said Andrei. "I'm just going for a smoke, okay?"

"Don't worry about it," Abel said gloomily.

When the heavy door with the deeply scratched graffito – "Locomotive are Champs" – and the filthy little window clicked shut behind him, he remembered he'd run out of cigarettes the day before. Fortunately, just behind the door he saw a tumbler-gambler, sitting in the middle of a small group of people. He begged a 'Mainline' from one of them and watched.

The tumbler-gambler was so old and wrinkled, he looked like a half-dead monkey, and an empty beer can for alms would have suited him far better than the three small plastic cups that he moved slowly around a piece of cardboard. Perhaps he was a guru and teacher – his large assistants were certainly very impressive and physically well-endowed: there were two of them, dressed in identical reddish-coloured jackets made by Chinese political prisoners from poor quality leather. They argued all too convincingly with each other, pushed each other in the chest and took turns at winning new fifty thousand rouble notes from the tumbler-gambler, who handed them over without saying a word or even looking up.

Andrei moved away and leaned against the wall by the window. The radio had guessed right – it really was a sunny day. As the tumbler-gambler raised his head and his bald patch gleamed in the slanting yellow rays, for a moment his remaining tufts of grey hair were transformed into a glowing halo, and the complex passes he made above the sheet of cardboard seemed like a ritual from some forgotten religion.

"Hey!" said one of the assistants, raising his head. "What's with all the smoke? There's no air left in here as it is."

Andrei didn't answer.

"You deaf?" asked the assistant, drawing himself up to his full height.

Again Andrei said nothing. Whichever way you looked at it, the assistant was in the wrong – it wasn't his territory.

"I turn and spin, I want to win," the tumbler-gambler suddenly wheezed.

This was obviously a codeword, and the assistant got the message. He tossed his head and went back to arguing with his partner. Andrei took a last drag and threw the butt at their feet.

His turn in the toilet queue had just arrived. Abel had disappeared, and the only person in front of Andrei was a woman carrying a baby. They were unexpectedly quick.

Closing the door behind him, Andrei turned on the tap, and glanced at his face in the mirror. In the last five years, he thought, rather than maturing or growing old, it had simply gone out of style, along with flared trousers, transcendental meditation and Fleetwood Mac. The fashion just recently was for quite different faces, in the spirit of the pre-war years – an observation which left considerable food for thought. However, Andrei left the thoughts to feed for themselves, cleaned his teeth, had a quick wash and went back to his compartment.

Petr Sergeievich was already awake and sitting at the table, scratching himself here and there as he leafed through an old copy of *Route* – Andrei had got it from a gypsy the day before for a can of beer, but hadn't actually read it yet.

"Good morning, Andrei!" said Petr Sergeievich, and pointed at something in the newspaper. "It says here the existence of the abominable snowman can be regarded as proved."

"Good morning, Petr Sergeievich," said Andrei. "It's a load of nonsense. You snored all night again."

"That can't be true. It isn't, is it?"

"Yes, it is."

"Did you try whistling?"

"Of course I did," answered Andrei, "over and over again. A waste of time. As soon as you turn on your back, you start snoring, and nothing makes the slightest difference. You should tie yourself down so you lie on your side all the time. You know – the way you did last year?"

"I remember," said Petr Sergeievich. "I was younger then. I can't get to sleep like that any more. What a pain. It's my nerves, Andrei. You know, I never used to snore before these fucking reforms. Never mind, we'll think of something."

"What else do they say?" Andrei asked, nodding at the newspaper.

Petr Sergeievich's thoughts had to be given a definite direction, otherwise he would go on reminiscing about the way things were before the reforms. Petr Sergeievich ran his finger across the greenish page, swearing monotonously as he paraphrased the leading article, and Andrei nodded and asked questions as he began thinking over his plans for the day. First he would go and get breakfast, and then he had to pay a visit to Khan, who had some obscure business to discuss with him.

The restaurant, a long narrow room with a dozen cramped little tables, was still empty, apart from a smell of burning. Whatever it was that burnt must have already been rotten, Andrei thought, as he sat in his usual place by the window, with his back to the cash desk. He looked at the menu, screwing up his eyes against the sun: there was nothing but millet porridge, tea and Azerbaijanian cognac. Andrei caught the waiter's eye and nodded. The waiter gestured as if he was holding something small – maybe a small glass of something – between his thumb and finger, and smiled inquiringly. Andrei shook his head.

Watching the hot sunlight falling on the tablecloth covered with sticky blotches and crumbs, Andrei was suddenly struck by the thought of what a genuine tragedy it was for millions of light rays to set out on their journey from the surface of the sun, go hurtling through the infinite void of space and pierce the kilometres-thick sky of Earth, only to be extinguished in the revolting remains of yesterday's soup. Maybe these yellow arrows slanting in through the window were conscious, hoped for something better – and realised that their hope was groundless, giving them all the necessary ingredients for suffering.

"Maybe I seem just like one of these yellow arrows falling on the tablecloth to someone," he mused to himself, "and life is nothing but the dirty window that I'm flying through: and here I am falling, falling for God knows how many years already onto the table, right there in front of the plate, while someone looks at the menu and waits for breakfast..."

Andrei looked up at the television in the corner and caught a fleeting glimpse of a face soundlessly mouthing something into three brown microphones. Then the camera swung round and showed two figures jostling furiously at another microphone, clutching each other's identical red ties in a shameless exhibition of Freudian frenzy.

The waiter came over and put his breakfast on the table. Andrei looked into the aluminium bowl at the millet porridge and the blob of melted butter resembling a small sun. He didn't feel like eating, but remembered he wouldn't be back here again before evening, and began stoically swallowing the lukewarm gruel.

The first customers appeared, and the restaurant gradually filled up with the sound of their voices – Andrei had the feeling that the silence hadn't actually been broken, it was simply that a few distracting irritants had been added to it. The silence was as thick and sticky as the porridge in his bowl; it distorted the voices, which sounded jerky and hysterical against its background. At the next table they were talking loudly about the abominable snowmen – apparently some crazy old woman had seen one the day before. Andrei tried listening to the conversation for a while, and then gave up.

The seat opposite him was taken by a florid-faced, grey-haired man in a severe black jacket with small silver crosses on the lapels.

"*Bon appetit*," he said with a smile.

"Give me a break," said Andrei.

"Why so gloomy?" his companion asked in surprise.

"What makes you so merry?"

"I'm not merry," replied the other, "I'm joyful."

"Well, then," said Andrei, "I'm not gloomy, I'm thoughtful. I'm just sitting here meditating."

He finished his porridge, moved his glass of tea closer, and began stirring the sugar. His companion continued to smile. Andrei thought he was about to start speaking again, so he began swirling his spoon faster.

"Of course, thinking, and even sometimes meditating", said his companion, waving his hand like a conductor, "is useful, in fact, very often necessary in life. But everything really depends on where the process originates, so to speak."

"You mean there are different places?" asked Andrei.

"Now you're being ironical, but in fact there are. Sometimes a man will try to solve a problem that was solved thousands of years ago, but he simply doesn't know it. Or he doesn't realise that it is his problem."

Andrei finished his tea.

"Maybe," he said, "it really isn't his problem."

"All of us actually have the same problem. It's only our stupid pride that won't allow us to admit it. A person, even a very good one, is always weak if he's alone. He needs support, something that gives his life meaning. He needs to see the reflection of the supreme harmony in everything he does. In what he sees around him day by day."

He pointed at the window. Andrei looked out and saw a forest, and far beyond it, at the very horizon, three huge rust-brown chimneys from some power-station or factory, towering up into the sky. They were so broad they looked like gigantic tumblers. Andrei laughed.

"What's wrong?" asked his companion.

"You know," said Andrei, "I just had this vision of a huge drunken guy with a mouth-organ, tall as the sky, but really stupid and unsteady on his feet. He's playing away at some stupid song, the harmonica's all shiny with grease. And when someone down below notices him, it's called a reflection of the supreme harmony."

His companion frowned.

"You know, there's nothing new in all that," he said. "A hierarchy of demiurges, an incomplete and monstrous world and so on – if the historical parallel interests you. Gnosticism, in a single word. But it will never make you happy, you know."

"I'm sure it won't," said Andrei. "All those frightening words. But what will make me happy?"

"There is only one path to happiness," his companion said authoritatively, scraping his spoon in his bowl. "To find meaning and beauty in all of this and submit to the great plan. Real life only begins after that."

Andrei felt like asking just whose plans one should submit to, and which of them exactly, but he thought his companion was sure to answer this question by forcing some brochure or other on him, and he kept quiet.

"Maybe you're right," he said, rising from the table. "Thanks for the conversation. I'm sorry, I'm always in a bad mood in the morning. I can see you're a very well-educated man."

"It goes with my job," said his companion. "Thank you. Please accept this small keepsake."

He held out a small coloured brochure. On the cover was a

picture of an improbably pink ear, and flying into the ear was a twelve-calibre, metal musical note with wings. It was gleaming brightly – clearly in reflection of the supreme harmony. Andrei thanked his companion, stuffed the brochure into his pocket and walked to the door.

He was in no hurry, but he walked quickly all the same, apologising every now and then as he bumped into one of the numerous people who were always wandering along the narrow corridors at this time of day. They were looking out of the windows and smiling, and spots of sunlight quivered on their faces. There was an unusually large number of young but already bloated women in Turkish tracksuits with silent, fidgety children busy with the unsystematic study of the external world. Sometimes, too, they were accompanied by men with their vests hanging over their pants, many holding cans of beer in their hands.

Andrei felt that the new day had already swept him up in its current and was forcing him to think about all sorts of things which didn't interest him at all. But there was nothing he could do about it – the voices and sounds from the surrounding space penetrated unhindered into his head and began tumbling around inside there, like the balls in a lottery drum, becoming for the time being his own thoughts. At first everything was filled up with the infernal jingles pouring out of the concealed speakers, then they started broadcasting the weather forecast, and Andrei began casting sideways glances at the windows drifting by, beyond which the south wind was supposed to grow stronger. Several times he had to squeeze by groups of people clustered round the travelling altar of one of the tumbler-gamblers – it was really amazing the way all the tumbler-gamblers and their assistants looked the same – they even spoke with the same southern accent, as though they belonged to some special community whose children all learned the art of squeezing a polystyrene pea under their thumb nail and shuffling three inverted plastic cups around a piece of cardboard. A few minutes later, Andrei finally stopped in front of a door covered in yellow plastic, with the number "XV" and a scratch-mark that looked like an arrow pointing upwards.

Khan was alone; he was sitting at the table drinking tea and looking out of the window. He was dressed, as usual, in a black tracksuit with the inscription 'Angels of California' – which always raised some doubt in Andrei's mind about the angels of that particular state. Andrei noticed that Khan had not shaved for a long time, and he looked like Toshiro Mifune working his way into a new role, especially since a touch of mongoloid blood gave him the same slanting eyes.

"Hi," said Andrei.

"Hi. Lock the door."

"What if your room-mates come back?"

"They won't," said Khan.

The nickel-plated lock made a loud click. For an instant Andrei had a sense of foreboding: the sound of the lock reminded him of the click of a gun-breech. But then his alarm suddenly seemed ridiculous.

"Sit down," said Khan, nodding at the seat opposite him.

Andrei sat down.

"So what's new?" asked Khan.

"Nothing much," said Andrei. "Did you ever wonder where the last five years went to?"

"Why five?"

"The exact number doesn't matter," said Andrei. "I said five because I personally remember myself five years ago as being just the same as I am now. Wandering around the place in just the same way, looking things over, thinking just the same thoughts. Another five years will go by, and everything will be just the same, don't you see? Why are you looking at me like that?"

"Come on," said Khan, "get a grip."

"I didn't think I'd lost my grip."

Khan shook his head.

"Tell me now, quickly," he said, "what is the 'Yellow Arrow'?"

Andrei looked up in surprise.

"That's strange," he said. "Today in the restaurant I was thinking about yellow arrows. Or not really about yellow arrows, more about life. You know, the tablecloth was dirty, and the sunlight was falling on it. I thought..."

"Get up."

"What for?"

"Get up, get up," repeated Khan, rising from the table.

Andrei rose to his feet and Khan took him rather roughly by the collar and shook him several times.

"Do you remember what you came here for?" he said.

"Let go of me," said Andrei. "Are you crazy? I just dropped in, that's all."

"Where are we? What can you hear?"

Andrei pulled Khan's hands off his jacket and gave a puzzled frown, then he realised he could hear the regular rhythmic hammering of steel on steel, which had been there all the time, even though he wasn't consciously aware of it.

"What is the 'Yellow Arrow'?" Khan repeated. "Where are we?"

He turned Andrei to face the window, and Andrei saw the tops of the trees hurtling past the window from left to right.

"Well?"

"Hang on," said Andrei, "hang on."

He clutched his head in his hands and sat down on the bunk-bed.

"I remember," he said. "The 'Yellow Arrow' is a train travelling towards a ruined bridge. The train we're riding in."

10

"Can you recall now what happened to you?" asked Khan.

"Not very well," said Andrei. "Not in detail. It's as though nothing unusual really happened. I knew what my name was, and which compartment I was from. But it was as if that wasn't me at all. I felt very strange – as though it made some kind of difference which carriage you rode in. As if everything that happened would make more sense if only the tablecloth in the restaurant was clean. Or if the T.V. showed different faces – you know what I mean?"

"No need to explain," said Khan. "You simply became a passenger for a while."

Andrei turned away from the window and glanced at a panel on the wall of the carriage lobby, which held two dusty dials and the words "check every...".

"I'm a passenger right now," he said. "And so are you."

"A normal passenger never thinks of himself as a passenger," said Khan. "So if you know you're a passenger, you no longer are one. They could never imagine that it's possible to get off this train. Nothing else exists for them, apart from the train."

"And nothing else exists for us apart from the train," Andrei said darkly. "If we don't deceive ourselves, that is."

Khan laughed. "If we don't deceive ourselves," he repeated slowly. "If we don't, we'll only be deceived by others. And anyway, the ability to deceive what you call 'myself' is a great achievement, because usually that 'self' is what is doing the deceiving. It doesn't matter in the least whether anything else exists apart from our train. What matters is that we can live as though there is something else. As though it really is possible to get off. That's the only difference. But if you try to explain that difference to any of the passengers, they won't understand."

"Have you tried, then?" asked Andrei.

"Yes, I have. They can't even understand that they're riding in a train."

"It's all nonsense," said Andrei. "Passengers who don't even realise that they're riding in a train – people would think you're crazy!"

"They just don't understand. How can they understand something they already know so well? They don't even hear the sound of the wheels any more."

"That's true," said Andrei. "I know that myself. When I went into the restaurant I even thought – how quiet it is when the place is empty."

"You see! Nice and quiet. You can even hear a spoon clinking in a glass. Remember, when a man stops hearing the sound of the wheels and just wants to keep on moving, he becomes a passenger."

"Nobody asks us whether we want to keep moving," said Andrei. "We can't even remember how we got here. We're travelling along, and that's all there is to it. There's no choice."

"There is, but it's the most difficult thing in life. Riding in a train without being a passenger," said Khan.

The door of the compartment opened and the conductor

came in. Andrei recognised his companion from the restaurant – only now he was wearing a uniform cap, and the jacket with the silvery spanners or crossed hammers gleaming on the lapels, now hung open across his protruding belly to reveal a scarlet pullover worn over his black uniform shirt. He was absent-mindedly winding round his hand a piece of string with the symbol of his office – a key in the form of a small nickel-plated cylinder with a handle shaped like a cross. It could be used as a knuckle-duster in encounters with drunken passengers – or as a bottle-opener. The conductor also recognised Andrei. He gave him a broad smile and touched three fingers to the peak of his cap in salute.

"What's he grinning at?" asked Khan, when the conductor moved off down the carriage.

"Nothing. We got talking in the restaurant. What do I do if it happens again?"

"What?" asked Khan. "You mean with the conductor?"

"No. If I turn into a passenger again."

"You simply have to stop being one, that's all. It happens to all of us."

"What does that mean, to all of us? How many of us are there?"

"A lot, I think," said Khan. "There must be a lot, only we don't know each other. There certainly used to be a lot."

"Tell me, who was it first told you about all this?"

"I don't know," said Khan, "I never saw them."

"What do you mean? How could you learn something from someone you've never seen?"

"That's the way it was," said Khan, and Andrei realised he wasn't going to talk about it.

"But where are they now?" he asked.

"I think they're out there," said Khan, nodding towards the window, which was filled with an endless, drifting expanse of fields overgrown with grass that rippled in waves like water in the wind.

"They're dead?"

"They got off. Some night, when the train stopped, they opened the door and got off."

"Seems to me you're getting things mixed up," said Andrei.

"The 'Yellow Arrow' never stops. Everyone knows that."

"Listen," said Khan, "just think for a moment. The passengers don't even know what the train they're riding in is called. They don't even know that they're passengers. So what can they know?"

9

As soon as Andrei opened the door of his carriage, he realised that something had happened. Several men in dark suits were standing by the door of one of the compartments: an elderly woman in a black shawl was crying. The radio was not working, but there was depressing music playing on a small tape recorder in the compartment where Abel lived. Andrei went into his own compartment.

"What's happened?" he asked Petr Sergeievich.

"Soskin's died," said Petr Sergeievich, putting down his book. "It's the funeral."

"When did it happen?"

"Last night. They're moving someone from the waiting list into Abel's compartment."

"That's why he was in such a miserable mood," said Andrei. He looked at the book Petr Sergeievich was reading: it was Pasternak's *Early Trains*.

"That's right," said Petr Sergeievich. "Things didn't work out like he wanted. He tried to fix it so his brother could move in. You know the way it is, one greasy wop gets his foot in the door, and then he moves the whole family in. But when the senior conductor took a look at the documents, he said: he's already got a berth in a compartment, and we've got lots on the waiting list in the open carriages. Not that I believe he'll actually move anyone in here from an open carriage. Abel just didn't slip him enough. Or he slipped it to the wrong man, so he was sent packing."

Andrei suddenly remembered he still hadn't bought any cigarettes.

"What's the book about?" he asked.

"About life, I suppose," said Petr Sergeievich.

He returned to his reading.

Andrei went out into the corridor. They were just carrying the body out of the compartment, so he stopped by the window – it wasn't done to push your way past a group of mourners. In any case, the ceremony didn't usually drag on for too long.

The pale profile of the dead man appeared in the doorway above the edge of a sheet of hardboard held by two con-ductors. The hardboard, which was kept specially for this purpose, was painted red on both sides with a black border, so that it looked like a flag of mourning; for some reason, it had come to be known as an 'ash-tray'.

The body was covered up to the neck with an old scarlet blanket. Abel appeared from somewhere and began struggling to open the window – it wouldn't give, and two other men came to his assistance. Together they pulled the window-frame downwards, opening up a gap of about forty centimetres. At this, the woman in the dark shawl began weeping loudly, and people took her by the arms and led her back into the compart-ment. The conductors carefully raised the board, pushed its edge out through the window and began to ease the body out – they did everything slowly, in order not to offend anybody's feelings by undue haste. At one point the body almost got stuck, when the blanket on his chest snagged against the frame.

Standing where he was by the window, Andrei could see the dead man's head with its hair flapping wildly in the wind – it was skimming along three metres above the embankment, the half-closed eyes staring up at the sky, which was gradually filling up with blue-grey clouds. As it moved out from the yellow wall of the carriage, the head jerked a few times, then began to bend down towards the ground. The scarlet edge of the blanket fluttered past the window, and there was a dull thud. A moment later a pillow and a towel flew past the window: it was a tradition that they were always thrown out after the body.

Andrei could have gone to buy cigarettes now, but he went on standing there, looking out of the window. Several seconds went by, then suddenly the green slope came to an end, the hammering of the wheels against the joints in the rails became louder, and the rusty beams of a bridge began to rush past the window as the train crossed the wide blue expanse of an unknown river.

8

There was music playing in the restaurant, the eternal cassette that always ended suddenly half-way through 'Bridge Over Troubled Waters'. Andrei spotted his old friend Grisha Strupin at one of the tables, dressed in a fashionable tweed jacket with the winged insignia of the Ministry of Railways pinned to his lapel – it cost a huge amount of money, but Grisha could afford it. When the communists were still in power, he used to do a bit of trade in cigarettes and beer along the corridors of the carriages, and now he'd expanded into really big business. Sitting opposite Grisha was a close-cropped foreigner, eating caviare mixed with the boiled buckwheat in his aluminium bowl. Grisha noticed Andrei and beckoned him over, and a moment later Andrei squeezed into the free place beside him. Just recently Grisha had become even more plump and jolly, and his hair was curlier than ever – or perhaps it just seemed that way because he was already a little drunk.

"Cheers," he said. "This is Andrei, a friend from my sinister childhood. And this is Ivan, a friend of my mature years and business partner."

"So the guy's an emigré, come back home again," thought Andrei. They shook hands without speaking. Andrei looked around to see if he could spot any familiar faces. There weren't any, although, as usual in the evenings, there were plenty of drunken Finns and Arabs.

"Have a drink?" asked Grisha.

Andrei nodded, and Grisha poured three large glasses of 'Railroad Special' from the carafe on the table.

"To our business!" said Ivan, raising his glass. He drained it and gave a heavy sigh. "Ah, yes, Grisha, I forgot. There's this big batch of toilet paper, with Saddam Hussein's portrait. It was remaindered when demand fell after the war, and it's real cheap. What would it be worth here?"

"It might be worth a lot," said Grisha, "but I can tell you straight off there's nothing to be made on it. The real market for toilet paper is very limited – just the first-class compart-ments. It's not worth the effort."

"What about the seating carriages and the open carriages?" asked Ivan.

"It's never been an item in the seating carriages, and now with inflation the way it is, the open carriages are changing to newspapers too."

"Alright," said Ivan, "so much for the open carriages. But what about the compartments. Or don't the people there?.."

"For the time being, sure," said Grisha. "But it makes no difference to us. I tell you, there's no room there for anyone new to squeeze in."

"Why not?" asked Ivan. "If you're selling cheaper?"

"How can I do that, Ivan? You should spend a bit less time on theory. If I sell just one roll cheaper, they'll chuck me out through the window alive. I tell you, we can't do anything."

"We can't spend all our lives dealing in cigarettes and beer," said Ivan, lighting up a cigarette. "We've got to move on to something bigger. Did you check out the aluminium?"

"Yes," said Grisha. "Seems like it's a real proposition."

"What's the scheme?" asked Ivan.

"Currency-roubles, then currency-currency-currency," said Grisha.

Ivan screwed up his eyes for a moment, as though he was looking at something blindingly bright in the far distance.

"Aha!" he said, then he took a small calculator out of his pocket and became absorbed in juggling figures.

"What kind of scheme is that?" Andrei asked Grisha quietly.

"What a question! You pay the senior conductor, and he writes off the spoons. This guy's serious – he only takes currency. The one condition is you have to break the spoons, because they won't let whole ones past the border lobby, and anyway, they can cause problems. So you need breakers. They take roubles, about ten per cent of what the senior conductor gets. That's the currency-roubles part. Then you have to pay currency another three times – in the staff-car, at the border lobby, and protection money."

"And how does he work it out?" whispered Andrei,

nodding at Ivan. "How does he know how much to pay every-one?"

"They print the rates every day," said Grisha. "For buying and selling. Don't you know anything? Seems to me like the real world left you behind a long time ago. Still thick with that Khan of yours, are you? Tell me, is that his real name or his nickname?"

"It's his real name," said Andrei. "And if you're interested, his nickname is Brake Handle."

"What's that mean?"

"It's a thing on a boiler," said Andrei, "to let the steam escape. He used to work with a boiler."

"God," said Grisha, "a boilerman. You'd be better off making friends with the waiters."

Ivan raised his head.

"It's okay," he said. "Let's go for it. What about the copper?"

"That's not so easy," said Grisha. "In theory it's the same scheme, but all the ash-trays have inventory numbers. You need a separate authorisation for each one written off. That means you have to pay the assistant senior conductor on top of everyone else, and I don't have any direct leads on him. I've spoken to one of his secretaries, but he's very cagey. As soon as I mentioned ash-trays, he was out of there like a shot."

"Did you at least run the idea past him?" asked Ivan.

"Not yet. Seems like he's not a player."

"Okay then," said Ivan. "Get started on the spoons tomorrow, and we'll decide about the copper later."

He got up, said goodbye politely, and went towards the door. Grisha watched him go and then turned to Andrei.

"I visited him recently," he said. "Just imagine, only three compartments in the whole carriage, and a bath in every one. The standard of living..."

"What's that mean?" asked Andrei. "The standard of living?"

"Don't be silly, Andrei," Grisha said with a frown. "One thing I can't stand is when you pretend to be stupid. Let's have a few more drinks instead."

"Okay. Only tell me, honestly, aren't you afraid of dealing

in ash-trays?"

Grisha was about to open his mouth to reply, but a sudden thought struck him and he half closed his eyes to focus on it. For a few seconds his face was a frozen mask, while his curly hair flapped wildly in the stream of air from the open window.

"No, I'm not afraid, Andrei," he said at last. "And I won't let anything put the wind up me."

7

"Khan," said Andrei, "won't you tell me how you could learn something from someone you've never even seen?"

"You don't have to see a man in order to learn something from him. You could get a letter from him."

"Did you get a letter like that?"

Khan nodded.

"Can you show it to me?" asked Andrei.

"I can, but it means a long walk."

The further they went, the more run-down the open sleeping carriages became, and the filthier the curtains separating the cramped and crowded bunk sections from the passageway. These places weren't entirely safe even during the morning. Sometimes they had to step over drunks or make way for the ones who hadn't yet tumbled over and fallen asleep. After that came the sitting carriages – strangely enough, the air here was cleaner, and the passengers they met also seemed cleaner and more neatly dressed. The men wore faded and patched cotton pants, and the women wore washed-out housecoats; the seats were divided off from each other by home-made screens, and the floor was spread with newspapers covered with playing-cards, egg-shells and slices of bacon fat.

In one carriage they were singing songs to guitars in three different places – in fact it sounded like they were all singing the same song, 'Train on Fire', only different parts of it at the same time. One group was just beginning, another was finishing, and a third was ploughing drunkenly through the chorus, but with the wrong words.

"By the way, about letters," said Khan, as he ducked under

one more string of washing. "You've received plenty of them yourself. You could even say you get them every day. And so does everyone else."

"I don't get your meaning," said Andrei. "I personally have never received any letters."

"Have you ever wondered why our train is called the 'Yellow Arrow'?"

"No, I just took your word for it."

"Think about it."

The voices behind the bright-coloured curtains gradually changed until they spoke with a distinct southern accent. After a prison carriage where an armed guard in a padded uniform and cap marched up and down in front of locked doors, they moved on into incredibly crowded sitting carriages, a mixture of rubbish tips and gypsy camps, crawling with dirty gypsy children. And then came the empty carriages – they said people used to ride in them once, but now there were only bare bunks scarred by pen-knife graffiti, and bullet holes and burn marks on the walls. Half of the windows in them were broken, and the holes let in a cold wind. The floors were covered with garbage – old shoes, newspapers and broken bottles. Andrei was just about to ask how much further they had to go, when Khan turned to him and spoke.

"We're almost there," he said, "at the next lobby. So tell me, why is our train called the 'Yellow Arrow'?"

"I don't know," said Andrei. "It's probably something mythological. Perhaps at night, when all the lights are on, from outside it looks like a flying arrow. But then there'd have to be someone who'd seen it from outside and then come back into the train."

"It's not only from the outside that it's like an arrow."

They emerged into the lobby. Khan stepped to the left without speaking and opened a door to reveal the gaping maw of a rusty stove and a curving pipe with a pressure-gauge, on which hung a bone-dry rag. The last carriages before the border had been without hot water for a long time, and the stove looked as though it hadn't been lit for maybe ten years, since the very beginning of Recoupling.

"In the corner," said Khan, "on the wall. Light a match."

Andrei squeezed into the dark narrow space and struck a match. There were words scratched on the wall, very old and hard to make out. Written in block capitals, they made up several sentences arranged in a column, like verse:

"*He who has cast off the world has likened it to yellow dust.*"

"*Your body is like unto a wound, and you are like unto a madman.*"

"*This entire world is a yellow arrow which has pierced you through.*"

"*The yellow arrow is the train on which you ride towards a ruined bridge.*"

"Who wrote this?" Andrei asked.

"How should I know?" said Khan.

"But you must have some idea?"

"No," said Khan. "It doesn't matter, anyway. I told you, there are letters all around us – it just takes someone to read them. For instance, the word 'earth' is another letter with the same meaning."

"Why?"

"Think about it. Imagine yourself standing at the window looking out. Houses, kitchen gardens, skeletons, mileposts – in a word, everything the intellectuals call 'kilture'."

"Culture," Andrei corrected him.

"Yes, and most of this 'kilture' consists of dead bodies mixed up with bottles and bedsheets. In several layers, with grass on the top. This is also called 'earth'. The stuff that bones rot in, and the place where we live are called by the same name. We're all inhabitants of earth. Beings from the next world. You understand me?"

"Yes," said Andrei. "Of course I do. Tell me, did you ever think about where we're travelling from? Where this train started?"

"No," said Khan. "That doesn't particularly interest me. I'm interested in finding out how to get off. You ask the conductors. They'll tell you where the train came from."

"Yes," said Andrei thoughtfully, "they'll do that alright."

"Shall we go back?"

"I'll stay here for a while. I'll catch you up in five minutes."

When Khan went out, Andrei turned towards the window. It was the first time he'd been in these carriages, and now that there was no one around, unusual thoughts came to his mind, thoughts he'd never had in the restaurant, though everything necessary for them to appear was there too.

What he saw when he looked back through the window – a section of embankment relieved by a bush or a tree that was hurtling away into the past – was the point where he had been a second before, and if the carriage he was riding in was the last, then there would be nothing at that point except emptiness and branches swaying at both sides of the tracks.

"If everything that existed a moment ago did not disappear," he thought, "then our train and we ourselves would not look like we do. We would be spread out through the air above the sleepers. We would be like a tangled bunch of snakes, surrounded by endless ribbons of plastic, glass and steel. But everything disappears. Every past second disappears, with everything that was in it, and no one knows what he will be like in the next. Or whether he will still be there at all. Or whether God will grow tired of creating one second after another, with everything that they contain. Nobody, nobody at all can guarantee that the next second will arrive. And the moment in which we actually live is so short that we cannot even grasp it, all we can do is recall the previous one. But then what actually exists, and what are we?"

Andrei caught sight of his own transparent reflection in the glass, and tried to imagine it disappearing, and another appearing in its place, and so on to infinity.

"I want to get off this train while I am alive. I know this is impossible, but I want to do it, because to want anything else is sheer madness. And I know that the phrase 'I want to get off the train while I am alive' does have a meaning, although the words which make it up have no meaning. I don't even know who I am. Then who will leave this place? And where will he go? Where can I go to, if I don't even know where I am – at the point where I started to think this, or at the point where I finished? And if I tell myself that I am here, where is this 'here'?" And what does it mean, 'I tell myself'?"

He looked out of the window again. It was almost dark

already. Every now and then, clearly visible in the twilight, white mile-posts loomed up at the side of the tracks, looking like small stone sentries.

6

Andrei opened the latest copy of *Route* at the centre page, where the most interesting articles usually appeared, under the heading "Rails and Ties". A title in thick print ran right across the top of the page: FUNDAMENTAL ANTHROPOLOGY.

He settled himself more comfortably, folded the newspaper double and began reading:

"The rhythm of wheels which accompanies each of us throughout life from birth to death is, of course, the most familiar of all sounds. Scientists have calculated that the languages of various peoples contain about twenty thousand imitations of this sound, of which about eighteen thousand belong to dead languages; the majority of these forgotten sound-combinations cannot even be reconstituted because the remaining records are too meagre, or as yet undeciphered. However, the imitations that exist in modern languages are, of course, both varied and interesting – some anthropologists regard them as elements of metalanguage, or cultural 'code words', which allow people to identify their carriage-fellows. The longest of these is the expression used by the pygmies of the Cannabis plateau in Central Africa, which sounds as follows:

'Oo-koo-le-le-oo-koo-la-la-o-be-o-be-o-ba-o-ba'.

"The shortest of these auditory representations is the plosive 'p', which is used by the inhabitants of the upper reaches of the Amazon. The following is a list of the way wheels sound in various countries of the world:

"In America, 'ginger ale-ginger ale'. In the Baltic countries, 'pa-duba-dam'. In Poland, 'pan-pan'. In Bengal, 'choong-choong'. In Tibet, 'dzog-chen'. In France, 'clicot-clicot'. In the Turkic-language countries of Central Asia, 'bir-sum', 'bir-som' and 'bir-manat'. In Iran, 'avdal-haladj'. In Iraq, 'jalal-iddi'. In Mongolia, 'ulan-dalai'. (It is interesting to note that in Inner Mongolia, the wheels sound quite different, 'un-gern-khan-

khan'). In Afghanistan, 'nakshbandi-nakshbandi'. In Persia, 'beel-zebub'. In Ukraine, 'trikh-tararukh'. In Germany, 'vril-schrapp'. In Japan, 'dodeska-zen'. Among the Australian aborigines, 'tul-up'. Among the mountain tribes of the Caucasus and, typically, also among the Basques, 'darlan-bichesyn'. In North Korea, 'uldu-chu-chkhe'. In South Korea, 'duldu-kvan-um'. In Mexico (especially among the Ouichotl Indians), 'tonal-nagual'. In Northern China, 'tsao-tsao-tan-tien'. In Southern China, 'de-i-chan-chan'. In India, 'bhai-ghosh'. In Georgia, 'koba-tsap'. In Israel, 'taki-bats-buber-boom'. In England, 'click-o-click' (in Scotland, 'gluck-o-clock'). In Ireland, 'bla-bla'. In Argentina..."

Andrei looked down to the very bottom of the page, at the short paragraph following the long columns filled with lists:

"But of course, the sound of the wheels is most beautifully, most movingly imitated in Russia – 'out-there – out-there' (in some remote areas also 'down-there'): the rhythm seems to point the way to some bright distant dawn stirring us to the very depths of our souls..."

There was a knock at the door. Andrei automatically grabbed for the handle, and nearly fell off the toilet seat.

"Will you be much longer?" asked a voice in the corridor.

"I'm just coming," said Andrei, and he crumpled the newspaper into an untidy ball.

"Out-there, out-there," sang the wheels under the filthy wet floor. "Out-there, out-there, out-there, out-there, out-there".

There was a hold-up in the next carriage because of a funeral. They were letting people past, but the crowd was moving very slowly, and it got stuck for long periods.

"Badasov's died," said a voice somewhere nearby.

Standing in front of Andrei was a fidgety little girl with huge dirty bows in her hair. She was banging her fist on the window as she looked out, turning round every now and then to her mother.

"Ma," she asked suddenly, "what's out there?"

"Out where?" asked her mother.

"Out there," said the girl, and she banged her fist on the window.

"Out there's out there," said her mother with a bright smile.

"Who lives out there?"

"Animals do," said her mother.

"And who else is out there?"

"There are gods and spirits out there," said her mother, "but nobody's ever seen them."

"Don't people live out there?" asked the little girl.

"No," answered her mother, "people don't live out there. People ride in a train."

"Where's best," asked the little girl, "in the train or out there?"

"I don't know," said her mother, "I haven't been out there."

"I want to go out there," said the little girl, and she tapped her finger on the glass.

"Wait for a while," her mother said with a bitter sigh, "you'll be out there soon enough."

The drunken conductors finally won their struggle with the 'ash-tray', the body thudded onto the ground, bounced and tumbled down the embankment. Out after it flew a cushion, a towel, two red wreaths and a marble paper-weight – to judge from all that, the deceased must have been someone important.

"I want to go out there," the little girl wailed to a non-existent tune, "out there, out there..."

Her mother tugged at her hand, put a finger to her lips and made wild eyes as she nodded at the crowd of mourners. Noticing Andrei watching the little girl, she raised her eyes to his face and arched her brows slightly, as though inviting him to share in her condescending amusement at such childish naivety.

"Why are you looking at me like that?" Andrei asked the woman. "Maybe I want to go out there too?"

"You mean, to join the abominable snowmen?" she asked.

Andrei recalled the tracks he had seen in the snow outside the window of the restaurant a year before – they were clearly the tracks of shoes, stretching alongside the railway lines for several dozen metres, and then suddenly breaking off, as though the person who made them had vanished into thin air.

5

The lamp over the table was on, and Petr Sergeievich was smoking his evening cigarette, dropping the ash neatly into an empty glass. He always dragged on the cigarette with a slight expression of disgust, as though he was kissing a woman he no longer loved, but didn't wish to offend by neglecting her.

"They should be put away," he said. "I tell you, the swines should be put away."

"Who?" asked Andrei.

He was lying on his bunk-bed with his hands behind his head and staring at a black dot that was crawling across the ceiling.

"All of them," said Petr Sergeievich, for some reason switching to a whisper. "The entire staff carriage, starting with the senior conductor. Just look what's going on. We got used to having no spoons, okay. But now it's the ash-trays. Where are the ash-trays, eh? You tell me that."

"They must have been stolen, I suppose," said Andrei.

"And who stole them?" screeched Petr Sergeievich. "They're not just thieves any more. We used to have thieves who stole things, but this is a different business altogether. They're selling off the Motherland, that's what."

"Oh, come on," said Andrei. "You weren't born in any ash-tray."

"D'you think I'm worried about the spoons and the ash-trays? It's the young girls I feel sorry for, our pure girls, those blue-eyed does who have to sell themselves to all sorts of scum in the open carriages. Understand?"

Andrei said nothing.

"Bare-faced banditry," said Petr Sergeievich in a calmer voice. "They're not afraid of anything. They've got the authorities in their pocket."

"There never was a time when they didn't steal things here," said Andrei. "At least this lot don't throw people out of the windows while they're still alive."

There was a loud knock at the door of the compartment.

"Who is it?" asked Andrei.

"Andrei, it's me," someone shouted on the other side of the

door. "Open up quick!"

It was Grisha's voice. Andrei jumped to his feet and opened the door. Grisha slipped inside and immediately locked the door behind him. There was blood on his face and a few patches of it on his jacket. Andrei noticed that the winged insignia of the Ministry of Railways was gone from his lapel, and in its place was a jagged hole.

"What happened?" he asked, sitting Grisha down on the divan.

"I got mugged," said Grisha. "I left the restaurant, on my own, and I was almost home, and then – can you imagine? – it was in the passage between carriages. Four of them attacked me. Two in front and two behind. One of the bastards had a sharpened spoon."

"Did they get much?"

"A lot," he said, "don't ask. Ivan settled up today and they took the lot. Bastards. Petty amateurs."

Andrei moistened a cotton towel with water from the carafe and held it out to Grisha.

"Why?" he asked. "Didn't you pay up on time?"

"What's that got to do with it?" said Grisha, pressing the towel to his temple. "It was just some gang of muggers. Only they don't know who they've come up against. I'll make things hot for everyone around here tomorrow."

"Maybe someone put them up to it?"

"No way," said Grisha. "Apart from Ivan, nobody knew a thing about it. And he'd have no reason. I tell you, it was just some gang."

At this point, Petr Sergeievich, who had been discreetly concealing his face behind his newspaper, peeped out and said:

"You see, Andrei, you see? You say they don't throw people out of the windows any more? Well, they ought to. Just the way they used to – tie their hands and feet and throw them out onto the sleepers head-first. In public. Then we'd have sugar in our tea, and people would behave in the corridor. And no one would dare to touch your friend here."

"And you're not afraid they might throw you out?" Andrei asked.

"Me? What for? I've worked honestly all my life. You just

take a walk through the compartment carriages – half the doors are fitted with these handles. Whoever's in power, they need me."

"Doors?" said Grisha, suddenly coming to life. "Excuse me, what's your name? Pleased to meet you, Petr Sergeievich. I'm Grigory Strupin, director of the joint venture 'Blue Carriage'."

Petr Sergeievich shook the hand extended to him, smiled and straightened his collar.

"I apologise for my appearance," said Grisha, smiling broadly with his bloody mouth, and looking askance at his ruined lapel. "An unfortunate incident. At present I just happen to be in need of some professional advice about doors. For a fee, of course – we can draw up a contract later."

"Well, if I can be of assistance..." said Petr Sergeievich.

"Tell me, are the locks on the doors really made of nickel?"

"No," said Petr Sergeievich. "They're only plated with nickel. The locks themselves..."

"Listen, Grisha," said Andrei. "You carry on talking here, and I'll take a walk along the corridor to see if there's anybody waiting for you."

He closed the door behind him.

The corridor was deserted. Andrei reached the end and glanced out into the lobby – there was no one there. It was the same at the other end of the carriage. Returning to the door of his own compartment, he could hear Grisha talking excitedly and Petr Sergeievich humming and hawing evasively. He stood outside the door for a few seconds and then walked on further along the carriage. He stopped beside a plexiglass holder on the wall and took out a booklet. On the cover was a portrait of the author, a man with a moustache who looked like a much thinner, wiser and more sober version of Nietzsche, and the booklet was called *A Guide to the Railways of India*. About half the pages were missing, crudely ripped off the staples. Andrei stopped in the well-lit space before the lobby, rested his foot on the triangular lid of the rubbish bin, leaned against the window and began to read the page that would have been next to leave the booklet:

"... advised by His Reverence Shri Livmilon, I asked myself the question. The answer came almost immediately – all of my conscious life, the thing I have loved most of all is to stand by an open window in the corridor with my arms outside and my foot on the triangular lid of the rubbish bin, watching the wall of the jungle rushing past. Sometimes I have to press my shoulder against the glass to let people through into the lobby, and then I remember that I am standing at the window of a carriage hurtling across India, but all the rest of the time I am not really aware what is happening and to whom. Have you not noticed, dear reader, that when you look at the world for a long time and forget about yourself, nothing is left except what you see: a low slope covered with thickets of hemp (which people begin to gather with special sticks as soon as the train slows down), a line of palms twined round with lianas, separating the railway from the rest of the world, occasionally a river or a bridge in the colonial style, or an empty road defended by the steel arm of a boom. Where do I go to at such times? And where do these trees and booms go to when nobody is looking at them?

"What does it matter to me? There is something else far more important. I am closest of all to happiness – although I won't attempt to define just what it is – when I turn away from the window and am aware, with the edge of my consciousness, that a moment ago I was not here, there was simply the world outside the window, and something beautiful and incomprehensible, something which there is absolutely no need to 'comprehend', existed for a few seconds instead of the usual swarm of thoughts, of which one, like a locomotive, pulls all the others after it, absorbs them all and calls itself 'I'. Once again the trumpet call of an elephant in the distance, no doubt a white one – this is happiness..."

"Hey!"

Andrei looked up. Grisha was standing in front of him.

"Well? Did you see anyone?"

"No," Andrei answered. "But you'd better stay in the compartment for another half hour just in case."

"No," said Grisha, "I'll go. Your neighbour turned out to be a pretty useful guy. I've set up a meeting with him for tomorrow. See you."

"See you."

Grisha disappeared behind the door of the lobby. Andrei closed the brochure, stuffed it into his pocket and went back to his compartment.

Five minutes later, when the light was switched off, and Andrei was struggling hard to fall asleep before Petr Sergeievich could begin snoring, Petr Sergeievich unexpectedly cleared his throat and asked:

"Tell me, Andrei, why does Grisha call you a mystic? Is he joking?"

"Yes," said Andrei, "of course he is. He's the biggest mystic we have around here."

4

As always, Andrei was woken by the radio – a boundless baritone reciting poetry:

"She lies and stares as if still living
From the embankment ditch out there
A lovely girl with coloured kerchief
Tied loosely round her braided hair.
The train went rumbling on as usual
Its coaches juddering and creaking,
First class and Second were silent
Third class was filled with songs and weeping..."

Petr Sergeievich was still snoring. Andrei glanced out of the window. The sky was low and grey, and it was misty with rain – the small drops splattered against the glass.

There was a knock at the door.

"Come in!"

The conductor brought in their tea. He put the glasses on the table, picked up the hundred-rouble note and closed the nickel-plated lock of the door behind him with a click.

The click woke Petr Sergeievich. Instead of turning back to face the wall and go to sleep for another couple of hours as usual, he sprang up and supported himself on his elbow, staring at Andrei with a crazy expression on his face.

"You were snoring again last night," said Andrei.

"Yes? Did you whistle?"

"Of course I did," answered Andrei.

"What time is it?" asked Petr Sergeievich.

"Half past nine."

Petr Sergeievich swore, leapt to his feet and began hastily combing his hair; Andrei now saw that he'd slept in his suit, complete with a tie.

"Where are you off to in such a hurry?" asked Andrei.

"Business," said Petr Sergeievich, shoving under his arm a worn leather briefcase that Andrei hadn't seen him touch for three years, and dashed out into the corridor. Andrei turned to face the wall and closed his eyes. The poetry on the radio was over, and the announcements had begun. Andrei turned the volume control anti-clockwise as far as it would go, but the voices were still clearly audible.

"All of us look forward to a better day," sang a children's choir, "as the Blue Carriage goes rolling on its way." "The 'Blue Carriage' company," proclaimed an excited contralto voice in follow-up, "Our train is a real express!"

That was Grisha's advertisement. Then the speaker gave out a squeaking noise, and a jolly male voice announced: "Try a 'Combat' cigarette – it's the greatest feeling yet." Then there was a long pause, followed eventually by 'Morning Cinema'.

"Today we shall be discussing Japanese director Akira Kurosawa's film *Dodeskaden*," the announcer said in a nasal voice. "Made in 1970, the film is based on a short novel by Akutagava Riunoske, *The Rhythm of Invisible Wheels*. In fact, the very title of the film in Japanese is a representation of the sound of wheels hammering against the rails. So close your eyes and imagine it is early morning in a post-war Japanese compartment carriage. Doors are banging as people hurry out into the corridor on their way to work. The famous sun of Japan is shining brightly outside the windows darkened by the smoke of recent battles. Suddenly, there among the crowd, is the first of the film's heroes, the one who is known in his carriage as 'the tramcar madman'. This young man imagines that he is the driver of an invisible small train – a 'tramcar' in Japanese – which runs to and fro in the real carriage. A concept, I'm sure you'll agree, which is far from simple and requires some effort to grasp..."

Andrei got up and began to dress quickly. When he had his jacket on he fastened all the buttons, took his sunglasses and peaked cap down from the upper bunk, and then put the gloves and small wooden wedge he kept under his mattress into his pocket. While he was getting dressed the radio was barely audible, but when he halted for a moment in the doorway, wondering whether he'd taken everything he needed, he heard the insinuating, nasal voice once again:

"... it must be admitted that the heroes of the film are occupied with genuinely important and serious matters – small-scale wholesale trade, slow death by starvation, theft, child-birth and so forth. And so, in drawing a parallel between the life of these people and the actions of the 'tramcar madman', who runs up and down the corridor of the carriage, shouting 'dodeska-den! dodeska-den!' in imitation of the rhythm of the wheels of his imaginary train, Kurosawa is, as it were, attempting to show that each of his socially adjusted heroes is in effect travelling around the real carriage in his own little imaginary 'tramcar'. However, Kurosawa fails to indicate any way out of the stark, comfortless world he shows us. What point is there in simply alarming people, and then..."

The radio was not on in the corridor.

Andrei was lucky, he only had to go two lobbies in one direction before he found himself in a completely empty corridor. To judge from the smell, they had been poisoning the cockroaches, and the passengers had taken shelter from the odour behind closed doors. Andrei walked quickly along the dusty carpet, and halted beside the door of the service compartment, where the conductor was humming as he hunched over the huge metal sink and washed empty beer cans – in the next carriage they painted them in a folk-art style and sold them to the West. Andrei waited for a moment when the conductor was looking the other way, slipped past his door and went into the toilet. He locked himself in, forced the wedge between the door and the lever of the lock, and hammered on it several times with his palm – now not even the conductor could open the door from the outside with his key.

The window opened straight away. Andrei glanced through

the gap – all the windows nearby were closed. He put on the gloves, the cap and the dark glasses, turned his back to the window and felt with his outstretched hands for the upper rim of the frame. Then he braced his foot against the metal handle on the wall, doubled over and began slowly and cautiously working his way outside.

He knew all the movements so well he could perform them with his eyes closed, but even so every time he had a few moments of anxiety. In the occult books that they sold in the lobby by the restaurant, the procedure was described in a very confused and mysterious fashion, full of allegorical phrases – the books were obviously written by people who didn't really know what they were talking about. The simplest euphemism used for the process was the expression 'ritual death'. In a certain sense it was that – the same thing happened to dead people who were pushed out of the windows onto the embankment. But that was the only similarity, even though the procedure actually was quite risky. As for the dark subconscious fear, the only means to combat that were a clear head and a sense of humour – Andrei reminded himself that he was simply climbing on to the roof of the carriage.

Above the window there was a hollow gutter to drain away rain from the roof. Andrei grabbed hold of its rim and pulled himself up until he was sitting on the edge of the window with his legs dangling inside the carriage. Far ahead, he caught sight of a strip of green bushes, and he started climbing more quickly, to avoid being lashed by the branches. A few seconds later he was up on the ribbed and strangely wide roof of the carriage, covered with flaking yellow paint and punctuated by the rusty protruding mushrooms of the ventilation turrets. He stood up and looked around.

A long way to the west there were people standing on the roof, but he couldn't make out any faces. Andrei jumped over the gaps between several carriages until he found a dent which told him that he was above Khan's carriage, and he stamped on the roof.

Khan appeared about five minutes later, wearing an oil-skin jacket with a hood and the same kind of glasses as Andrei. They set off towards the west without speaking, running up to leap over the gaps above the rubber passageways that linked the carriages.

Soon they were past the slippery roof of the restaurant and the carriage with the border-guard lobby, and the people up ahead began to wave their hands in greeting. Andrei recognised several of them and he waved back. He didn't actually know any of them in the usual sense – all communication with the people that he and Khan met up here consisted entirely of an exchange of gestures. They walked past an old man in a dirty padded jacket and an old military fur hat – as usual, he was sitting motionless with his legs crossed in the centre of the roof and smoking a long-stemmed pipe with a tiny metal chibouk (it was a mystery how he managed to light it in the wind). Further on there was a group of people sitting in grey cassocks – their faces were hidden by hoods, so it was impossible to tell what age they were, or whether they were men or women. They sat in a circle, studying an incomprehensible geometrical figure traced on the carriage roof in charcoal. The figure was the same as it had always been – a circle with a symmetrical design like an open star. Andrei recalled that the previous summer, and the summer before that, they were doing the same thing, but he had no idea what their purpose was in gazing at this simple drawing for so long.

In general, Andrei doubted that the people he met on the roof climbed up there with any particular purpose in mind. He himself had never had any such purpose, and he didn't expect anything from these outings. True, it was here that he first met Khan. That time they hadn't exchanged a word – nobody ever spoke to anybody else up here – but they recognised each other in the corridor a couple of days later. Khan said later that climbing out on to the roof was probably not only pointless, but positively harmful, because it only removed you even further from any real chance of leaving the train – but he still went on climbing up there, simply in order to get away for a while from the stifling communal space of life and death. Neither the beginning nor the end of the train were visible – in both directions the line of carriages extended to the very horizon, curving several times on its way, but nonetheless, somewhere there was a locomotive. Apart from the numerous

arguments of metaphysical speculation which went on in the
carriages below, there were two direct proofs of this – the thick
copper cable half a metre above their heads, and the long low
rumbling sound that could sometimes be heard from an invisible source.

Andrei felt Khan tug at his sleeve, and then looked where
he was pointing. On the roof of the next carriage there was a
rather strange group – four people dressed up like musicians, in
exaggerated Latin American costumes. A moment later Andrei
noticed the instruments in their hands and realised that they
actually were musicians. The clattering of the wheels made it
quite impossible to hear the music, but he could see the small
orchestra was putting everything they had into it – the one with
the pan pipes was squatting down as he played, and the
guitarists' faces were so frenzied, they might have been holding
rifles instead of guitars. They looked as though they were
storming Pablo Escobar's armoured carriage. Looking beyond
them, Andrei saw a strange figure with a broad-rimmed straw
hat hanging at his back – he was standing dangerously close to
the edge of the carriage, dancing on the spot and waving his
arms about as though he was trying to keep warm. Andrei had
never come across this man or the musicians up here before.

The train was rushing at speed towards a river, or perhaps
a narrow offshoot of a lake, spanned by a strange bridge with
very low barriers that barely came up to the roof of the train.
The thought occurred to Andrei that you could probably jump
over them – and at that very moment the man with the hat on
a string pushed off hard from the roof of the carriage and went
flying over the barrier.

For a few seconds, Andrei could not believe it had really
happened. Then he dropped onto his belly, crawled to the edge
of the roof and hung over it in an attempt to see something.
The water under the bridge was practically motionless; there
were circles spreading across the surface, and bobbing up and
down at their centre like a huge water-lily was the hat. A few
long seconds later a head came bobbing up to the surface like a
black football. The man swam to the water's edge, and then a
grassy embankment hid the entire scene from view.

Andrei rose to his feet and looked at Khan. He was shaking

his head in admiration and his lips were moving as though he was saying something. Everybody nearby was looking back towards the river they could no longer see – even the incomprehensible group in the cassocks, who usually paid no attention to the others, were standing and gazing, perplexed, towards the East, where the stranger had left them forever. Only the old man in the fur hat carried on sitting motionless in his usual spot, releasing barely visible spurts of smoke into the wind – Andrei couldn't tell whether he simply hadn't noticed anything, or whether he'd seen it all before. The musicians had disappeared. Andrei looked around for them and spotted several small figures jumping from one carriage to the next, already quite a long way to the horizon.

3

"Like it?" asked Anton. "Be honest."

"What?"

"The new series," said Anton, nodding towards the table.

"What series?" asked Andrei. "They're all the same."

"That's the concept," said Anton. "They're numbered, like lithographs."

Andrei was sitting on the edge of the bunk-bed, looking at the beer can that Anton was painting. Anton muttered quietly as he traced a small brush over the surface of the can, bending his neck in an unnatural manner in order not to get paint on his beard, but despite this, there were already several white blobs on it, looking like patches of prematurely grey hair. Several painted cans stood on the table, all with the same design: the corridor of a carriage with rosy-cheeked girls in traditional Russian costumes carrying glasses of tea, and flaxen-haired youths in red peasant shirts, all with the same face, like a cow's udder.

"Well?" Anton asked again.

"I think it's good," said Anton. "But there's too much social comment. 'The Lord's Budweiser' was much better."

"I don't understand," said Anton, "why everything I paint has to be compared with the 'Budweiser'."

"It just came to mind," said Andrei. "It was a really

brilliant piece."

Sitting opposite Anton was his wife Olga, who was cleaning down the cans with fine sandpaper. Her legs were covered with a blanket because the door of the compartment had been taken off its hinges, and there was a strong draught across the floor. Another blanket hung in place of the door, but it didn't reach down to the floor, and they could see the shoes and slippers of people walking along the corridor. Andrei looked up at the bent hinges and shook his head.

"I can't understand why you allowed them to take the door down," he said. "Nobody had any right to do it if you didn't agree."

"Nobody asked us if we agreed or not," said Anton. "They just came and told us it was Conversion. From compartments to open carriages. They gave us something to sign, and that was that. I don't want to talk about it. Have you seen any of our friends around recently?"

"I see Grisha pretty often," said Andrei. "He's got lots of money now. And I saw Sergei just recently. He's changed a lot. Doesn't drink or smoke. He's become a bedeist."

"What's that?"

"It's a religion, a very beautiful one. They believe we're being pulled along by a 'B.D. 3' locomotive – sometimes they just call it a 'number 3', and we're travelling towards a Bright Dawn. Those who believe in the 'B.D. 3' will pass over the final bridge, but the others won't."

"Yes?" said Anton. "That's something I never heard of before. You don't happen to have accepted it, I suppose?"

"No, I haven't," said Andrei. "I haven't changed at all. I'm just reading this interesting little book I came across by accident. It's called *A Guide to the Railways of India*. I can lend it to you when I'm finished, if you like."

"What's it about?" Anton asked, lifting the beer can up over his head and scrutinising it.

"It's not so easy to describe. It's just this person riding across India in a train and writing about what happens to him. It's not even really clear whether he actually is riding across India or simply imagining it. You'd enjoy it."

"Have you got it with you?" Anton asked.

"Yes," said Andrei.

"Read me a bit, will you? My hands are covered in paint."

"Which bit?" asked Andrei.

"Any will do."

"Then," said Andrei, "I'll start from the part I'm reading myself. I can just sketch in what comes before – first he writes about what he sees through the window, and then he begins to describe the people who make it difficult for him to stand at the window – he gives a very long and bitter list of different types."

Andrei took the booklet out of his pocket, opened it at the bookmark and began to read aloud.

"Where are they all going? What for? Do they never hear the rhythm of the wheels or see the bare plains outside the windows? They know everything there is to know about this life, but they still just move on along the corridor, from the W.C. to their compartment, from the lobby to the restaurant, gradually transforming today into one more yesterday, and they think that a God exists who will reward them or punish them for it. But if they don't go insane, it must mean they all know some secret – or else I know a secret which it would be better for no one to know. Something which makes it impossible for me ever again to walk home so innocently and sense-lessly, with my eyes blank and empty, along the gently swaying corridor, and not even be conscious of the fact that it is me walking along the corridor. But I don't know any secret. I simply see life as it really is, soberly and accurately, and I can never mistake this yellow catafalque rattling over the joints in the rails for anything else. I like India, and that's why I'm riding through India just at the moment. But they are simply the mad passengers of a mad train, and all I hear in the words they speak is the clattering of the wheels. And the fact that there are many of them, and I am almost alone, changes nothing..."

Andrei heard a rustling sound, and looking up he saw Anton's wife putting on her boots. Anton was wiping his hands on a paint-stained rag.

"Sorry, old son," he said, "we're going to the theatre. Read us the very last line, so we know how it all ends."

Andrei hesitated, then he opened the last page and read:

"Mercy is unbounded, and I know for certain that when the train stops, waiting for me there outside the yellow door will be a white elephant, on which I shall continue my eternal journey back to the Nameless."

"I get it," said Anton. "It's interesting, of course. But I don't think I'll read it all the same, thanks."

"Didn't you like it?"

"I wouldn't say I either liked it or I didn't," answered Anton. "It just has nothing to do with me personally."

"Why? What about the things you paint?" said Andrei, nodding in the direction of the painted cans. "Aren't they the same things in a different language? Stop the carriage, and so on? Or are you not serious about it all? Not sincere?"

"What does that mean – not serious or not sincere?" asked Anton. "Childish ideas you seem to have. Life, now, and art – creative work – are not the same. There's soc-art and concept-ualism, there's modernism and postmodernism. I long since stopped confusing them with life out there. I've got a wife, and soon we'll have a child. That's really serious stuff, Andrei. I can paint anything I like, it's all just different cultural games. I only stop the carriages now on these empty cans – I have to think about my child, and he'll be riding on in this real carriage here. You understand?"

He tapped the floor with his foot and pointed at the wall.

"It's time to go," said Olga, pulling aside the blanket hanging in the doorway. "We'll be late."

"What are you going to see?" asked Andrei.

"'Armoured Train One-Sixteen-Five-Eleven'," said Olga. "The production's very avant-garde."

"Whose production is it?"

"Upper Bunk Theatre," Olga said. "Everything's all collec-tive and anonymous down there, so no one knows whose any production is. But in secret I can let you know Anton painted the scenery. Would you like to come along? You could get in there alright."

"No," said Andrei, "I'll call on Khan. I haven't been to see him for a long time."

"Yes, by the way, how is he getting on, down there?" asked

Anton. "Has he discovered himself yet?"

"Yes," said Andrei, "and lots of other things too. See you."

"See you. Be sure to say hello from us to everyone down there."

"Anton," said Andrei as they turned to go, "can you hear anything?"

Anton stood still and listened.

"No," he said, "not a thing. What should I hear?"

2

A calendar with a picture of kittens had appeared on the door to Khan's compartment, concealing the familiar scratch. For a few moments, Andrei struggled to grasp what had happened. He looked around to make sure he'd got the right door, then knocked. There was no answer.

Andrei opened the door. The compartment was in an incredible mess – the kind that only happens when there's a funeral or a birth or you move home. Sitting on Khan's bunk-bed was a stout woman well past her prime, whose puffy face still bore lingering traces of its former ugliness: age had merci-fully removed her from the zone of aesthetic classification. In front of her on the floor stood several suitcases and a basket covered with a shawl, which gave out a dense odour of sausage. A tiny child's leg clad in a white sock dangled over the edge of the upper bunk, swaying gently in time with the movement of the carriage.

"Hello," said Andrei.

"How do you do," replied the woman, looking up at him blankly.

"Where's Khan?"

"There's no one here by that name."

"You mean he's moved?"

"I don't know," she said, "maybe he's moved, or maybe he's died. We don't know. We were on the list and we got the space. Ask the conductor, he knows."

"What about his things?" asked Andrei. "Was there anything left?"

"There weren't any things here," said the woman in a

livelier voice. "Don't you go getting any ideas. There weren't any things."

"Don't worry," said Andrei, "I'm not accusing you of anything. I'm just asking."

"Nothing but an empty bunk," said the woman. "And the upper bunk was empty too. I wouldn't touch anybody else's things."

"I understand," said Andrei. He turned and pushed the door open.

"You're not Andrei, are you?" the woman suddenly asked.

"Yes. Why?"

"There was a letter lying around here addressed to Andrei, but it didn't say which Andrei. Maybe it's for you."

"It is," said Andrei. "Can you give me it?"

"It was somewhere around here," the woman mumbled, rummaging through the heap of clothes on the table. "It'll take months to sort all this out. Life's awful nowadays. Always a crush in the corridor – it's too much to cope with. Found it. There it is. Are you sure it's for you? Have you got your ticket with you?"

"Haven't got one," Andrei joked familiarly.

The woman giggled and held out the envelope.

"Save your dirty jokes for the young girls," she said skittishly. "That's all. There wasn't anything else."

"Thank you," said Andrei, putting the letter in his pocket. "Thank you very much."

"Goodbye," said the woman.

As he left the compartment, Andrei almost collided with the conductor walking along the carriage, but he didn't bother to ask him about Khan.

Petr Sergeievich was drunk and happy. The bottle on the table in front of him was not the usual 'Railroad Special', but a fancy cut-glass bottle of 'Blaze Away' cognac, with a locomotive fire-box on the label. Beside it lay some drawings and blueprints – Andrei noticed that one of them showed the handle of a door-lock, greatly enlarged. There were also some official looking papers with stamps – to judge from the greasy marks on them, they must have been wrapped round the salami that Petr Sergeievich had already savaged, the tattered remnants of which were scattered around the table as if they'd been pecked by an eagle.

"How are things?"

"Okay," answered Andrei. "How are you doing?"

Petr Sergeievich raised a large hairy finger.

"Tomorrow I'll be gone all day," he said, "from early in the morning. And I won't be back at night. Will you get my sheets for me?"

"Alright," said Andrei. "Just be sure to let the conductor know. Is it the thirtieth already?"

"Yes," said Petr Sergeievich, "time flies. Life could just pass you by. Have a drink?"

Andrei shook his head. He took off his shoes and lay down on his bunk-bed, turned to face the wall and took *A Guide to the Railways of India* out of his pocket. The letter was stuck between the pages. He hesitated for a moment, then stuffed the letter back into his pocket, leaving it until tomorrow. He opened the book at random.

"In essence, happiness does not exist, there is only the consciousness of happiness. Or, in other words, there is only consciousness. There is no India, no train and no window. There is only consciousness, and everything else, including ourselves, exists only in so far as it comes within its sphere. Why then, I wonder over and over again, why do we not move directly to an infinite and inexpressible happiness, abandoning everything else? Of course, we would also have to abandon ourselves. But who does the abandoning? Who is it that will be happy? And who is unhappy now?"

Andrei felt sleepy, and he found it hard to follow the words – they kept tumbling over each other as he looked at them, forming themselves into complicated geometrical tangles. He closed the book.

"Come on, Andrei," said Petr Sergeievich. "What's eating you? Have a gargle."

"I really don't feel like it, thanks," said Andrei.

"Please yourself."

Andrei turned over onto his back and studied the dull yellow lampshade attached to the ceiling.

"Petr Sergeievich," he said. "Did you ever think about where we're going?"

"What's the problem?" Petr Sergeievich asked through a mouthful of food. "Got girl trouble? No sweat. Dump one, pick one up. Down there in the general carriages. Takes your mind off all that stuff. Know how many of the little bitches there are, out there? Money's all it takes."

"All the same, where do you think we're going?"

"You mean you don't know?"

"Why don't you just tell me?"

"No reason."

"Then tell me. Where do you think we're going?"

"Where to, where to... Haven't you heard it all before? Everyone knows where to, where to. Towards a ruined bridge. Andrei, why fill your fucking head with all that bloody crap?"

1

It was a cloudy morning – the sky overhead had been replaced by a smooth grey surface like the ceiling in the corridor, but with no ventilation vents. Petr Sergeievich had already left. A note for the conductor lay on the table beside two glasses of tea that had gone cold. Andrei got dressed, took the letter out of his pocket and immediately put it back again. Then he locked the door and sat on the table. Petr Sergeievich couldn't stand this, and he would never have forgiven anyone for putting their feet on his bunk, but there was no need to worry about him today.

Andrei never missed a chance to spend a couple of hours alone by the window in the compartment. It was quite different from standing by the window in the corridor, where you constantly had to move to let people past and you had to interact with other people in all sorts of other indefinable ways. Andrei didn't really believe the author of the *Guide* when he wrote that you could devote yourself to serene contemplation of the landscape beside the doorway of a lobby crowded with people who were yelling and shouting.

It was not a very good day – an endless wall of trees was rushing by just a few metres outside the window. Such plantations usually obscured the view for several hours, or even days, and all you could do was watch the strip of grass between the train and the trees, and examine the items thrown out from the carriages of the 'Yellow Arrow' that had already passed by this way.

At first everything down below was fused into one long grey-green blur, but after a few minutes his eyes adapted, so it only took a split second to identify the foreign bodies in the landscape. Perhaps it wasn't his eyes that adapted, but his imagination – he didn't so much perceive the objects rushing past the window as reconceive and recreate what must be there, on the basis of the slightest hints offered by the outside world. Anyway, there could be no mistake concerning the majority of the objects lying on the slopes of the embankment.

The commonest, of course, were the empty bottles. In the winter they were bright green spots against the snow, but now he could only distinguish them from the grass by the way they glinted. The lighter beer cans were pulled down by the slipstream, so they didn't usually travel so far out from the carriages. Occasionally there were rather strange objects – in one small bog, for instance, there was a picture in an immense gold frame sticking up out of the mud. And then, about a kilometre after the picture, he glimpsed the remains of a nickel-plated samovar that had smashed to pieces when it fell. Close by lay a magnificent leather suitcase, with a large fat crow sitting on it. The bright white spots of used condoms were everywhere – sometimes you could confuse one with a small bone like a collarbone – and there were almost as many bones lying in the grass as bottles. Skulls were particularly numerous, probably because they were too heavy for the small rodents, and larger animals were afraid to come too close to the rumbling yellow wall. A few really old skulls had been polished a chalky white by the wind and rain, but the newer ones still had hair and pieces of flesh attached to them. Andrei was particularly amused by one skull wearing a gleaming spectacles frame, which seemed still to have lenses in it.

The bushes and trees were littered with the traces of recent funerals – towels of various colours, blankets and pillow cases. They fluttered in the wind like flags, saluting the new life rushing past and onwards; Andrei thought he remembered some poet had said that – afterwards he'd thrown himself head-first out of the window of the restaurant-car. There were plenty of pillows too, and by no means all new – some of them had already begun to rot in the frequent rain of that summer. Their owners usually lay close by, in the most varied poses and stages of decomposition: many of them had retained a dignified appearance even out on the embankment, their legs drawn up, one hand under their head, and the other arm stretched out along their body. There was a simple reason for this: sometimes, at the relatives' request, the porters would use string to tie the limbs of the deceased in some special pose, so that they looked decorous even in death – and it had something to do with religion too.

Andrei noticed there were more and more white flowers appearing in the grass by the embankment. At first he mistook them for condoms. Then he thought they were simply old flowers, until he saw that many of them were actually wrapped in cellophane, and lying with their stems upwards. Eventually bouquets began to appear, and then wreaths, all made of faded white roses. Andrei guessed what it all meant: about two weeks ago they'd shown the funeral of the American pop star Isis Schopenhauer on television (her real name, Andrei remembered, was Janet Midgely). It said in the newspapers that during the ceremony two tonnes of the finest white roses were thrown out of the windows – the dead woman had loved white roses more than anything else in the world. They were what Andrei could see as he pressed his face against the glass. For two or three minutes more the white spots on the grass grew thicker and thicker, and then he saw a marble slab flanked by steel sphinxes, lying in the grass. Fastened on to it with gold chains was poor Isis, already well bloated in the heat. The edges of the slab were covered with advertisements – 'Rolex', 'Coca-Cola' and something in smaller script – it looked like the trade mark of a firm that produced vegeburgers with the "real American taste". There were two small dogs sniffing around the slab; one of them raised his muzzle towards the train and barked soundlessly. The other swivelled his tail: a long strip of something bluish-red was dangling from his jaws.

"World culture takes a long time to reach us," thought Andrei.

In the evening, just as it was beginning to get dark, the wall of trees outside the window came to an end. At first they thinned out, then gaps appeared between them, and suddenly there was an open field with a road running across it. Several brick houses stood beside the road, their windows gaping black holes and their shutters wide open. In the distance an incredibly beautiful white church with a crooked cross drifted by like a hand raised to heaven – only the upper part was visible, the rest was hidden by the forest.

Then there was a long deserted platform – Andrei spotted an old set of false teeth lying in solitary isolation on the flat concrete. Close by was a pole bearing an empty steel rectangle, which had once held a board with the name of the station. A wall made of several concrete slabs flashed by, with a tall heap of rusty iron lattices towering up behind it, then everything was hidden once again behind a dense living wall of trees – those who believed in the abominable snowmen said they had planted these trees to prevent the eyes and minds of the passengers from penetrating too far into their world.

Someone knocked on the door, and Andrei jumped up from the table.

"Who is it?" he asked.

"Abel," said a bass voice. "Come on out here, they're giving out the sheets."

When Andrei finally made up his mind to open the letter, it was already dark, and the wall of trees was still drifting by outside. He turned away from the window, took the envelope out of his pocket, and tore off the edge. Inside was a carefully torn piece of graph paper, with several lines neatly written in ink:

"Is the past history of locomotion pulled on into the future? The past always used to be someone else's or your own. Looking backwards, things seem to have disappeared from sight. Where is the key held, and who can you show it to? The pounding wheels write our journey's story. The postscript is the squeaking of the door."

The letter wasn't signed. Andrei read it through again, turned it over in his hands, folded it and slipped it back into the envelope. Then he lay down on his bunk-bed, switched off the lamp above his pillow, and turned his face to the wall.

0

Something strange was happening outside the window, something Andrei had never seen before. The train was moving across a flyover separated by a low iron fence from the streets of a city. Outside, there were countless lights – streetlamps, the windows of houses, car headlights. But the strangest thing of all was that down below there were people, lots and lots of people. They were standing by the fence of the flyover, and when Andrei's window drifted past them, they began waving and shouting merrily. The city seemed to be celebrating some kind of festival – everyone he saw looked as though they hadn't a care in the world.

Andrei eventually began to feel oppressed by the weight of so many gazing eyes. He stood up and went out into the corridor. Outside the window on the other side of the carriage there was the usual unbroken wall of dark trees, and Andrei felt more comfortable. The corridor looked strange, somehow – the floor was covered with a thick layer of dust, the doors of all the compartments were wide open, and he could see the naked iron frames of the bunk-beds. At first Andrei was surprised and even frightened, but then he remembered that apart from him, there wasn't a single other soul on the train, and he felt calmer.

He wanted to read the letter again, and he drew the folded envelope out of his pocket. As he looked over it this time, the text seemed to acquire a different sense, one which he had not seen before:

"The past is the locomotive that pulls the future after it –
Sometimes this past might even not be your own –
You are travelling backwards and see only what has already disappeared –
In order to get off the train, you need a ticket –
You hold it in your hands, but who will you show it to?"

As he glanced over the neatly written lines, Andrei turned back to the door of his own compartment and put his hand on the handle of the lock. Suddenly he noticed a postscript at the very bottom of the page, a brief note in small writing that he hadn't spotted before – probably because it was below the fold in the paper.

At this very moment he realised he wasn't standing in the empty corridor, but lying on his bunk-bed and dreaming. He began to wake up, but in that imperceptible instant it took to awaken, he managed to read and remember the postscript, or rather, remember the words – in his dream they had some quite different meaning, which could not be forcibly dragged into the ordinary world, but which he had just enough time to grasp:

"P.S. The problem is that we are constantly setting out on a journey which is over a second before we get started."

Andrei switched on the lamp above his pillow, took out the letter and read it – there was no postscript at all. The place on the paper where he had seen the postscript in his dream was only marked by a few faint scratches, as though someone had tried to write on it with a dried-out nib.

Something was wrong. Something had happened while he was asleep. Andrei got up from the bunk-bed and shook his head, then suddenly realised that he was surrounded by a deafening silence. The wheels were no longer beating out their rhythm. He looked out, and in the square of light falling from the window he saw a motionless branch covered in large black leaves. The train was standing still.

When Andrei went out into the corridor, everything was the same as usual – the lights were on, there was a smell of tobacco. But the floor under his feet was not moving at all, and Andrei noticed he was swaying slightly as he walked along it. The door of the service compartment was open. Andrei glanced in and met the gaze of the conductor, who was standing motionless by the table, holding a glass of tea. Andrei opened his mouth to ask what had happened to the train, but then he realised the conductor couldn't see him. At first Andrei thought he was asleep, or he'd fallen into some kind of stupor, but then he looked at the glass in the conductor's hand and saw the piece of sugar suspended in the tea, and the motionless string of bubbles suspended above it.

He already knew what he had to do next. He strode over to the conductor, carefully thrust his hand into the hip pocket of his jacket, and took out the key.

He stepped out into the lobby, went over to the door and put the key in the round keyhole. It didn't go in very far, because the hole was stuffed with all sorts of rubbish. He turned it. The door creaked open, and the hard dried cigarette butts crammed into the cracks around it tumbled out. Andrei thought for a moment about going back to the compartment to collect his things, but then he realised that none of the things he'd left in the suitcase under the bunk-bed would be any use to him now. He stood on the edge of the ribbed iron step and stared into the boundless quiet darkness, out of which a warm wind bore a multitude of unfamiliar smells. Then he jumped down onto the embankment.

As soon as his feet hit the gravel that covered the sleepers, there was a hiss of compressed air behind him, and a second later the couplings between the carriages clanked as they stretched. The train set off and began slowly picking up speed. Andrei moved away a few metres and looked at the 'Yellow Arrow'.

From outside it really did look like a flying arrow of bright electric lights, fired by an unknown archer at an unknown target. Andrei looked at the point where the carriages appeared, and then at the point where they disappeared; on both sides everything was blank and dark.

He turned and walked away, not really thinking about where he was going. Soon he found himself walking on an asphalt road across an open meadow, and a band of bright sky appeared on the horizon. The rumbling of the wheels behind his back gradually faded, and soon he could hear quite clearly sounds he'd never heard before – a dry chirping in the grass, the sighing of the wind and his own quiet steps.

Moscow, 1993